T0158547

PARTHIAN BOOKS

Tilting at Windmills

New Welsh Short Fiction

PARTHIAN BOOKS

First published 1995 by Parthian Books
41 Skelmuir Road, Cardiff CF2 2PR

With the financial support of the Rhys Davies Trust

ISBN 0 952 1558 1 8

Printed and bound in the United Kingdom
Typeset in Galliard by JW.

British Library Cataloguing in Publication Data.
A cataloguing record for this book is available from
the British Library.

The publishers would like to thank the Welsh
Academy for the support and administration of the
Rhys Davies Contemporary Short Story Competition.

Ravi Pawar was educated at Llangatwg and University
College, Cardiff. He moonlights as a teacher in the
English Department of Whitchurch Comprehensive.
He is married and lives in Canton.

For Lewis Davies

Rhys Davies
1901-78

The son of a village grocer in the Rhondda, Rhys Davies attended Porth Intermediate School before moving to London in his early twenties with the intention of embarking on a writing career. Apart from a period during the Second World War, he lived almost entirely by the writing of novels and short stories. Despite not having entered higher education he committed himself to a study of the English and European Classics, especially the French Masters of the Short Story and Chekhov, whom he especially revered. He published sixteen novels, including *The Black Venus* (1944) and *The Dark Daughters* (1947) in addition to over a hundred short stories. His work is characterised by a great variety of subject matter, skill in creating moments and situations of high drama, grotesque humour and attention to significant detail.

'...the instinct to dive, swift and agile, into the opening of a story holds, for me, half the technical art; one must not on any account loiter or brood in the first paragraph; be deep in the story's elements in a few seconds".

'Summer comes, life changes.'
Anton Chekhov

Tilting at Windmills

JACINTA BELL

Jacinta Bell lives near Rhayader with her husband and three children. She has recently graduated from the University of Glamorgan M.A. Writing Course. She is now working on her second novel.

From a distance you can see the red tractor slide slowly northwards across the top of the hill. When it reaches the falling wall you can watch how it turns, half a circle, before travelling back south again. If you move in a little closer, glide above the ground with the buzzards, you can see the man inside the cab. Strong, rough hands resting on the murmuring gear stick. His foot pushes down the clutch and his hand grasps the lever pulling it sideways into a lower gear, ready to turn. He can't hear the birds or the tractor's engine. He's got headphones clasped to his ears, hearing the voice of a young man telling him how long the tailback at Junction 14 on the M6 is. The man in the tractor doesn't care. The M6 is beyond Tom's realm of experience, but he needs that voice in his ear, manic and urban; he needs the human contact.

It's giving him a headache though. All those humans with their weather reports, travel updates and love songs, marginalising him, excluding him from a world he'll never be part of. He's been feeling the tension build up in the back of his neck all morning, working its way across his forehead, lined by a frown as he squints against the unfamiliar sun. He'll stop in a minute, have some coffee. He's brought a flask up from the house. One more furrow then a break.

He looks behind, watching the soil rain from the cultivator blades like a waterfall in flood, and smiles. He never thought he could have worked this rocky earth to such a fine tilth. It had been worth all the effort, the ploughing, cultivating, harrowing, fertilising and now, today, last time over with the cultivator before planting. The others think he's mad, so much work for so little return, but what's a man to do ? Subsidies being cut back all the time, so many farmers selling off their sheep, giving up the land. And Tom with no wife to go out and earn a little extra.

He can see the bank manager's shrug as he hid behind the cliche. "I would if I could Tom, but my hands are tied. They won't let me extend your overdraft." With those words he'd squashed the dream. Renovating the outbuildings and making them into holiday cottages, there was good money to be had from tourists, but it couldn't be. Tom had to think again. A different strategy to ease his burden of debt. The idea had come to him with his father's death. It was something the old man had talked about, lying there drifting between lives. He told Tom how they'd ploughed up the hills above Newtown back in '41, planted seed potatoes, hardy plants, grown in troubled times for the War Effort. Now was the time to do it again. There'd been disease in the lowlands, in England. Last year's potato crop, ruined. The market was looking for new suppliers. They wanted disease-free potatoes grown high in the hills. Tom was their man. The price of potatoes had tripled.

He takes off his headphones and steps down from the cab. From up here he can see the windmills across the valley, paddles floating slowly round in the breeze. You got a better return on those things mind, than you'd ever get on seed potatoes. He takes off his jacket and drops it to the ground, then stretches, trying to get rid of that ache in his neck. His shoulders crack. Thirty seven years old and his body's already beginning to grumble at this life. Body and mind in harmony on that one. The last time he had a good look at his body was the day of his father's funeral, five months ago. They'd all come home then: John, Emrys, Sian and Glyn. Emrys all the way from California. Tom couldn't understand why. He'd never come when the old man was alive, so why bother coming back for the funeral.

'To make sure the old bugger's dead.'

Tom had nodded. The stiff leather belt, cracked and worn, still swung from that hook in the stable.

'Why don't you come over ?' Emrys had asked. 'Sell this old dump, start a new life. There's so much going on over there. It'd do you good.'

He couldn't know how much his words hurt. Where was the recognition, the respect, owed to Tom for staying on the farm ? The family had farmed the valley for two hundred years and it was Tom, youngest child, who'd taken on the obligation of the land, the care of his parents, while each of them had gone off to better lives. Even Sian. You'd have thought the daughter would stay close to home, but no, she left for London and stayed there.

He hadn't answered Emrys, just a faint smile before he turned away. How could he begin to explain the sense of responsibility he had, yoking him to this place? He knew Emrys wouldn't understand. A man with no worries. His bronzed arm, Rolex watch at his wrist, slung over the shoulders of his new girlfriend. Twenty two, long legged and blonde, Susie looked like something out of Baywatch.

That night he'd stripped naked in front of the mirror in his room and examined his own body, unfamiliar and unloved. The dark hair growing on his chest had crept over his shoulders and half way down his back, while the hair on his head grew only thin and wispy. His chest and arms were strong, muscular, that was good, yes, he liked that. But then he turned sideways, noted his belly protruding too far, the rolls of fat, like cradling arms pulling away from his back and down under his stomach. Tell-tale signs of his fondness for beer. His legs, covered in wiry black hairs, were too short, but strong and solid, tapering to bony ankles and heavy, earthbound feet.

He wanted a woman, needed a woman, but who would want him ? It was two years since he'd felt the soft flesh of another human being, luxuriated in her firm, experienced touch. He'd had to pay for it, of course. He'd have to pay for it now but didn't have the cash.

There was a time when he hadn't had to pay, when he'd had a woman of his own, but she'd gone to Cardiff, to train as a nurse. She'd promised they'd stay together, come home to him when she could, but it didn't happen that way. Her visits home became less frequent, and the fire in her touch cooled. He would have made do with that, with the indifference. His parents had lived like that for years, but Sharon wanted something more. She wanted passion. It was all a long time ago. So many people had left since then. Gone away. These days he reads the personal columns in the local papers, trying to guess whose lonely heart is whose.

The coffee is hot, searing his tongue as it slips from the plastic cup into his mouth. He can see the cars below heading up and down the valley to places where people queue and wait and jostle alongside one another. He can't see the river running alongside the road now the trees are coming out, and neither can he hear it, only the white roar of engines echoing up the valley reaches his ears. He looks across at the windmills, still turning. Old man Evans gets two thousand pounds a year for each turbine on his land, and he's got twenty two on site. Forty four thousand pounds a year for nothing. Easy money. He knew the figures well, carried them around with him. Forty four thousand pounds he wasn't getting because his own hill wouldn't get planning permission now. Too close to the other windmills. Evans had won the jackpot but paid a high price. Nobody spoke to him anymore. Jealousy and anger. They'd argued endlessly over the industrialisation of the hilltops. Why not Scotland ? They'd asked. Why not England ? They'd killed the coal industry in Wales, but still hungered after power for their new technologies.

His headache's getting tighter. The surface of his coffee reflects the sun; his eyes smart at the glare. The colours in the hills are changing from the grey and brown of winter to green and blue. It's a day for the seaside. Building sandcastles on the windy beach at Borth with laughing children he doesn't have. It may not be too late.

He drains his cup, shakes the drops of coffee out before screwing it back onto the Thermos. He'll get it finished today, the field, then he can plant tomorrow. He thinks of the potatoes chitting in huge trays in the old barn. He'd had to put a new section of the roof on for them. Translucent. Dark green shoots unfurling towards the light. Tomorrow he'll bury them in his soil, get the Morgan boy to help, then ridge them up, wait for them to sprout. When he goes home for a sandwich he'll have another look at them, take something for his headache, then back up here to turn the last bit. He might go into town tonight, get on the outside of a few cold ones, as Emrys used to say. See if Dai's still interested in those hound pups. Perhaps Mavis'll be behind the bar.

He heaves himself back into the cab and arranges the headphones over his ears. The radio's off and silence swallows him up. He sits frozen, holding onto the steering wheel for support, looking ahead but not seeing the crisp line of horizon where earth meets sky. He tries to push it out, fight back, and catches his breath as the hurt, so long kept at bay, attacks him. It comes rushing at him, all the days and years laden with tedium, worry and frustration, ambushing him, forcing him down.

Cry-baby, cry-baby. The words of his brothers taunt him from childhood, and from somewhere his mother's face, tired and bored, appears, *big boys don't cry.* But they do and he is. He's sobbing there inside his tractor. Anarchy. Behaving the way a farmer never should. His head crashes onto the steering wheel, the physical pain a relief from the torment in his mind. Water leaks from his eyes, nose and mouth, he's gasping for breath. *I am so lonely.* The words burn like a fever in his brain. He sees the picture of a farmer walking alone back to his empty cottage, the caption *Does anybody really care* ? hanging above his head and Tom can't remember the answer.

The sun's still climbing as Tom heaves and groans and bellows like one of his ewes lambing, but no one hears. There's too much to bear, he can't do it anymore. Something is broken. His seed potatoes are now no more than a madness.

If you're still standing there on the opposite side of the valley, listening to the hum of the turbine, the whoosh of the paddles swinging round, you might just make him out, stumbling and rolling towards the slate farmhouse down there, and you might think he's drunk, but you're wrong, he's not. Watch as the black door falls open.

Habit forces him to kick off his boots before struggling into the kitchen and pulling open the cupboard where his mother hid her hoard of aspirins all those years ago. Insurance against a slow bitter death in the event of a nuclear war that didn't come. They hadn't cleared them out after she died so suddenly that morning, ten years ago. Tom hopes they'll still work. Does medicine go off ? He scoops up bottles and plastic containers and takes them over to the kitchen table where he stands them up like soldiers. He fetches the remains of the whisky from the cupboard above the cooker, takes a clear glass from the shelf.

Action calms him, stilling the storm. He pulls off his jumper, more slowly now and sits at the table. He pours the whisky into the glass, the flow trembles, falls softly, then he sits making patterns with the tablets. So many different shapes, different sizes. He's surprised by the variety of colour and texture. Some tablets, once white, are almost yellow now, others are chipped and flaked or stuck together so the only way he can get them out is by breaking the bottle. Some cocooned in plastic and foil have survived the best, packaged to discourage people from overdosing on them. They cannot know how the challenge distracts him, removes him from his pain. Carefully he pushes them out one at a time. A single pill shoots out across the room, hitting the fireplace like a bullet, another hits the floor, but there, he has it now, knows just how hard to press. He puts some tablets on his tongue, still stinging from the coffee, puts the glass to his lips and swallows. His mouth burns but the whisky's warmth relaxes him inside, his chest and shoulders, arms and legs. His hand moves from the table to his mouth and back again, so many times, a mesmerising movement, and as the afternoon moves forward Tom knows that all will be well.

Outside, you'll notice how the sun has peaked and now falls again. The breeze has picked up and the turbines' wings spin, glinting in the light, a camera's shutter winking over and over through the window at the man lying broken on the floor.

Too Perfect

JO HUGHES

Jo Hughes has published work in a number of magazines and anthologies. She was born and raised in Swansea before moving to London where she worked as an art editor, designer and photographer for several years before returning home. She is currently studying for an M.A. at Swansea University.

The man and woman were standing side by side at the marina studying the new housing development on the other side of the water. He had been expressing surprise tinged with disgust at the sight of the red brick buildings with their gabled windows and arches and as he put it "post-modern gee-gaws". While she, having no knowledge of what had stood there before and no great opinion on architecture, said nothing.

Then into the silence that hovered between them he suddenly offered "Do you mind ?" and before he had finished asking, took her hand in his. In reply she gave a squeeze of assent, noting as she did how large and warm and smooth his hand was.

To a passerby it would have looked like nothing out of the ordinary. He or she, on seeing this man and woman by the water's edge, would assume that this hand holding was a commonplace event for them. But it wasn't. This was the first, the only time of any real physical contact between them.

Later, still awkwardly holding hands, each now afraid that letting go might signal some end to that which had not yet even begun, they made their way to the old Town Hall, once the home of commerce and council and now a centre for literature. This was the purpose of their trip, the reason why at seven that morning, she had stood at the window of her bedsit in Cambrian Street, Aberystwyth, waiting for the tin soldier red of his citroen to emerge around the corner.

Each had expressed an interest in visiting the Centre and

had behaved as if they were the only two people in the world with such a desire. That was why, uncharacteristically, he hadn't suggested the trip to the other members of his tutorial group. It was also the reason why she had omitted to tell any of her friends, why she had agreed to wake Ginny that morning at ten o'clock, despite the fact that she and Dr. Terrence Stevenson would be, probably, enjoying coffee and toast together in Swansea by then.

Terry, as he was known to colleagues and students alike, was a large man, over six feet, with large bones and large appetites, which now as he neared fifty expressed itself in his frame. He had once been lithe and muscular but his body had thickened with age. He blamed too many years at a desk, the expansion of his mind at the expense of an expanding behind. But he dressed well enough, choosing dark tailored jackets and corduroy or chino slacks, as well as the odd devilish tie which was about as subversive as he got. In colder weather, as on this grey October day, he wore his favourite black Abercrombie overcoat of a cashmere and wool mix. The coat hung well from the shoulders and had the effect of tapering his body, disguising its imperfections with a veneer of powerful authority and masculinity.

Claire thought he looked like one of the Kray twins in this coat of his and to her that signalled a sort of dangerous sexuality. She could not help but imagine herself engulfed in that coat, held willing captive in its soft folds.

Next to him, she looked tiny, even less than her five feet and a half inch. Claire had very long hair, grown in excess to compensate perhaps for her lack of height. It hung down, straight and sleek to her bottom and a great deal of her time was taken up with this hair: washing, combing and plaiting it before she went to bed each night. Most of the time she wore it loose and her gestures, the movement of her head, body and hands were all done in such a way as to accommodate her river of hair. When eating, for example, she would hold the fork in one hand while with her other she held her her hair away from the plate. She was very proud of her hair and if asked which part of herself she liked the most, the reply would always be her hair. Her last boyfriend, whom she had met at the Fresher's Dance at college and dated for almost three years until the end of the final Spring term had loved her hair; had sometimes spread it over her naked body, Lady Godiva style when they made love; had once even made the pretence of tying himself to her by it.

Claire's body was like a boy's: flat chested and slim hipped. And today she was dressed like a boy too, with jeans and heavy black lace-up boots and a white shirt and a man's tweed jacket two sizes too big. Through both her right eyebrow and right nostril she wore tiny silver rings and her eyes and lips were exaggerated with make up in shades of reddish brown. She seldom smiled, but when she did her entire face was transformed into if not quite something beautiful, then something very like it.

They had trudged through an exhibition of artifacts relating to the town's one famous poet: the scribbled postcards, the crumpled snapshots, the yellowing newspaper clippings .all framed for posterity like the relics of some dead saint. Terry had begun by clucking and tutting yet more disapproval of the venture, disapproval he'd been nurturing and planning since he first heard of it, but with Claire by his side he found himself softening, growing acclimatised to her open minded acceptance of all such endeavours.

They spoke in whispers, though the place was almost entirely deserted, this being after all a grey Tuesday in October, and around the back beneath some engravings by Peter Blake they kissed their first kiss. It did not feel like the world's best kiss for either of them, but did well enough as an awkward, uncertain, snatched preliminary to better things. Afterwards Claire had wanted to wipe her mouth with the back of her hand, not from disgust but just because the kiss was a little wet. His mouth had swallowed hers, had not measured out the size of her lips yet.

After the kiss they each felt like a conspirator in some deadly plot; what they would create that day felt as if it might be as deadly as Guy Fawkes' gunpowder, as bloody as any revolution.

The second kiss came as they sat in a deserted bar of the Pump House. The barman, a student, they decided, was propped against the far end of the counter his head bent over a book. They took turns to guess what the book might be. Terry said it was a handbook about computing, and she thought it was the script of something like Reservoir Dogs.

The clock above the bar, a faux-nautical affair, hung with nets and cork floats and plastic lobster and crab, read twelve fifteen. They had the afternoon and the early evening to spend together. He was thinking about the Gower coast, a cliff walk, the lonely scream of wheeling gulls and the sea a grey squall bubbling under the wind. She was thinking about a hotel room, the luggageless afternoon ascent in the lift to the en suite room and the champagne, herself languishing on the sheets, feeling intolerably beautiful under his grateful gaze.

After that second kiss, which was prolonged, they wrenched themselves away and began to speak in a strange language of unfinished sentences and hesitant murmurings.

'Oh.'

'Gosh.'

'You know we...'

'I never...'

'Oh my...'

'We shouldn't...'

'I never thought...'

'Nor me...'

'I mean, I always thought that maybe...'

'Me too.'

Then they kissed again and the barman, who wasn't a student, raising his eyes briefly from his novel by Gorky, watched them with mild interest and though they made an odd pair.

The odd pair finished their drinks: pints of real ale. She stubbed out her cigarette and they made their way towards the exit, his arm thrown protectively around her shoulders while his broad back wore her tiny arm , its fingers clutching the cloth, like a curious half belt.

The sky looked by now, greyer and darker than before. To the West a blue black curtain advanced promising heavy rain and a wind blew up from the East sending her hair on a frantic aerial dance. They ran across the empty square as raindrops as big as shillings began to mark the paving stones with dark circles.

Then she half stumbled and he caught her and in catching her, gathered her to him and they kissed a fourth time, this the best, with the rain splashing their heads and water pouring down their faces.

When they had done with this, this their unspoken moment of willingness and promise and wilfulness, their pact to indulge in what they knew was an unwise thing, he quickly kissed the tip of her dripping nose and then hand in hand they began to run again.

Under the covered walkway, they slowed down and shaking off the worst of the rain from their hair and clothes, barely noticed a man standing close by. He was busy putting away a tripod and Terry muttered, "Afternoon" and the man, grinning broadly replied, "Thanks".

Naturally neither of them made much of this, assuming it to be yet another curious aspect of Welshness. A further example of the strange smiling politeness, the thanking of bus drivers and so on, the chatting to strangers which each of them had at first perceived as alien, but now despite their breeding accepted and in part adopted.

Later that afternoon, in his car near a field in the north of Gower, with the day as dark as ever they almost made love. The next day, back in Aberystwyth, they did make love.

She had rung him from the payphone in the hall of her house when she was certain all the other students had gone out. His wife had answered the phone and she'd given her the pre-arranged message which was that she'd "found the journal with the Lawrence article he'd wanted."

What happened that Wednesday was perhaps rather sad, though not necessarily inevitable. It became clear to both of them that they sought a fugitive moment; that there could be no more than this, the furtive opening of the front door, the climbing of the stairs, the single bed dishevelled and cramped under the sloping roof, his glances at his watch, her ears constantly straining for any sounds from down below. Both of them too tense for pleasure, but going through its rigours, him professionally, she dramatically.

Afterwards, when they had dressed again, they sat side by side on the bed like strangers in a doctor's waiting room each thinking silently about how to end it, how to escape. She took his hand and held it on her lap, then began to speak.

'Your wife...'

'Catherine?'

'She sounded...'

'Yes.'

'She sounded...'

'Nice?'

'She is. I...'

'I don't...'

'I can't...'

'I think that...'

'Me too.'

He sighed. She understood his sigh to mean that he didn't want to leave and she sighed back at the thought that he might cancel his three o'clock lecture in order to stay. He had sighed because he was wondering how long he ought to stay to make it seem at least remotely respectable. He rested his eyes on the small wooden bookcase next to her bed. She had all the required texts as well as a rather unhealthy number of books by and about the American poet Sylvia Plath. This made him sigh again. She was trying very hard to imagine him back in his study, with the coffee cups on the window ledge and the view of the National Library and the letter trays overflowing with student essays and she sighed again because now that she'd seen him in his underwear that seemed impossible.

He stood suddenly, ready to go, but somehow his watch had become entangled with her hair and she gave a yelp of pain as he unthinkingly yanked at it, ripping the hair from her head. They both looked aghast at the tangled clumps sprouting from the metal bracelet of his watch. He pulled at them but they cut into his fingers and stretched and curled and slipped and clung until finally they snapped leaving short tufts poking out here and there.

Tears had come to her eyes with the sudden pain. He looked at her and seeing this, with ill disguised irritation as much at himself as with her, said "I'm sorry," then bluntly, "Why don't you get that cut ?"

That would have been the end of the story, except that some moments elusive as they may seem when lived, come back in other guises unbidden. Theirs was a photograph, unfortunately a very good photograph of a young girl on tip toes, her long wet hair lifted wildly in the wind and a black coated man bent over her, his hands delicately cupping her upturned face as their lips met. Rain glistened on their faces and shone in silvery puddles on the paving stones at their feet and behind them the sky was a black brooding mass of cloud.

It was a timeless image, a classic to be reproduced over and over, whose currency was love, truth and beauty. The people who bought the poster and the stationary range and the postcard assumed that it must have been posed, that it was really too perfect.

An Evening with your Ex

DUNCAN BUSH

Duncan Bush is the author of a novel *Glass Shot*. He has published several collections of poetry including his latest work *Masks* which was awarded the 1995 Welsh Book of the Year. Born in Cardiff, he was educated at Warwick University, Duke University and Wadham College,Oxford. He divides his time between Wales and Europe.

No thanks, I said. Not for me. Coffee'll be fine. Long way to go back tonight. I was a long way, too, from taking anything for granted. And there was no harm in showing it, making the point early. And, driving aside, the rule's simple: it's okay to lose your head when all around you are losing theirs. That's the time to do it. But only then. You wouldn't go onto a squash court like that. So never have one, even one, when you're not sure where you stand. Whatever kind of situation it is. The tautness is your edge. Or all you'll ever have of one. Which is why I don't at lunchtimes, or if I stop off at The Malsters for an hour after work, with Jack or Andrew. Because there's no such thing as after work with people you work with. Things are too bloody tight around the office these days. It's a Perrier with a slice of lemon, thanks. I've got the car. Or, I've got a game tonight. And I never have one with a client. Never.

I lit a ciggy instead, while Kitty was in the kitchen. Third today. As soon as I'd shut the lighter, I wished I'd waited for the coffee. I smoked it as slowly as I could, but a ciggy is only so long, and she was making real coffee, I could hear it in the percolator. In my honour, so to speak. Like in the bloody advert.

Anyway, the best of it was gone by the time she came back with the cups. They were the speckly oatmeal ones from Ewenny pottery. She put mine down on the round table and took hers over to the sofa. She sat with the cup and saucer balanced in her hand, and tucked one leg under her.

So, she said. Big bright expression. Who you screwing these days ?

Great conversational openings of the world, I said. Number three thousand, nine hundred and fifty two.

It's a simple question, she said. It just, you know, flew into my mind.

I stubbed the cigarette. I shrugged. I told her about this girl in Finance and Planning, Lynne.

Nice, is she ? she said.

Yes, I said. She's nice.

Very nice ? Or just nice ?

Very nice, I said. I suppose.

How nice ? she said. How absolutely spiffing ?

Then she wanted details. Facts. Who ? What ? Where ? I.e. How much ? How often ? All the time as if all this might be no end of a novelty and amusement to her. I told her what this girl looked like. I said she was twenty six.

Going for a slightly later model this year ? she said. I shrugged. Married ? she said.

No, I said. Or if she is she hasn't told me.

Must be a nice change, she said. Again that so-sweet smile.

I didn't want to let her get into all that again, so I kept talking. Told her I'd been seeing this girl a couple of weeks or so. I made it sound a fairly casual thing. Stud bachelor existence in the nation's capital. The fifth floor's most eligible young executive, et cetera, Madison Avenue stuff. I had tried asking the girl out, so it wasn't difficult to colour in between the lines. I didn't want Kitty thinking I might be hard up or something.

I switched the subject as soon as I could. Started telling her about this and that at work, figures down on last year, talk of voluntary redundancies, accepting cuts in pay. Brendan Bell being offered early retirement. I knew she didn't really know a lot of these people. But you have to talk about something. I was feeling my way. I couldn't tell if she was bitter still. Or if this was just the way she'd made up her mind to handle everything from now on, the odd spiked comment and the one big smile. I didn't suppose she knew herself.

What I did know was she kept springing up out of the sofa for something. A couple of grapes from the bowl on the sideboard, then to brush the spat-out pips off her hand into the empty fireplace. To tip my ashtray into the bin in the kitchen with the ash and tip a single cigarette in it, or to get us both another cup of coffee, then more milk for hers. Then for a tissue from the box to wipe a smear of something on the polish of the tabletop she noticed in the light, or to wander out into the kitchen. All the time still listening, but with this bright malicious smile she'd set at a certain angle, like the hands of a clock. The whole thing was about as stylised as a bloody dance. And this, I knew, was in my honour too. To have me watch it sauntering around the room, the butch athletic act, the ex-Cyncoed bloody gymnast (P.E. and English, for God's sake). I used to hate the way she put that on sometimes when other men were there: the way she's sitting again abruptly now on that low sofa and throwing one leg over the other in those white training tights (and I mean tights) pulled up to just below the knee to show how brown her shins are. Me then looking somewhere else, not to seem to have been dogging her. Coveting her. My own wife.

I knew all this. But I knew this didn't necessarily mean or prove a thing, aside from making a point. Peacocks or bower birds we're not. The mating display and the big tease can be hard to tell apart.

Then, I don't know what happened, but I ran out of things to say. I just dried up. There was this silence.

You could count it. One. Two. Three. Four. We were looking at each other.

Then Kitty got up from the sofa, rose up out of it again, straightening one doubled-under leg. She came over. I was lying in the low chair. I was like a rabbit in a headlight. I thought she was going to drop between my open knees. That she would swallow me in one. She took a cigarette out of the packet on the table alongside me, stood there and clicked a light to it. She put the packet back, the lighter on top of it. I watched her swagger all the way back to the sofa.

Why have you started smoking menthol ? she said.

I cleared my throat. My mouth was spitless.

Because I don't really like them, I said. It helps.

She tried it. It's different, she said.

I looked towards the hole in the far wall. How's the conversion coming along ?

Not that I cared, even if it was still legally half my house. Not that I even really listened to what she was saying, how she'd knocked half the wall down ready and now the effing builder said he couldn't do the job till next month, he had so much work to finish. I was watching her smoke the cigarette instead: someone who rarely smoked one, concentrating on it so much, laying off the ash so carefully, so often, in her saucer. She's been phoning him up and trying to get a definite date out of him for weeks, she said.

He sends his wife to the phone. Soon as she hears my voice she says he's out. Of course I can see what he's doing. Making hay while the effing sun shines. Saving this up for the winter or a nice wet week. Nice cosy inside job.

I shrugged. Kitty seemed to be swearing more than usual. I think she's always thought that a woman using a certain amount of bad language is sexy. And perhaps she's right. (Even if that means leaving out all the times she's made me cringe by doing it at the wrong time, in the hearing of the wrong person.) I watched her taking that minty smoke down into her lungs again. For no reason. No reason at all. But like a schoolgirl, who smokes one on a big date. As if the cigarette was in my honour too.

I had to ask. I was afraid to. But I had to. I waited till she'd finished.

Anyway, I said. What about you ?

What about me what ?

Who are you screwing these days?

She laughed. She laid some more ash from the cigarette into the saucer. She had to flick it twice because she hadn't given it time to form.

Oh I don't know, she said. It varies. I might go down to the White Hart disco. Or to a Young Farmers do. Check out the talent. End up with a quick roll in the hay. With some broth of a boy who'll grow up into the usual overweight pig of a man you seem to get around here.

She gave the same laugh, which was harder than she was.

Oh, I said. Because what else can you say when you think of a thing like that?

She held the cigarette upright and watched the end smoulder. It was so close her eyes almost crossed. I have been seeing someone on a slightly more regular basis, she said. Or a slightly less random one, anyway.

I'd started this. It had to go on. Anyone I know ? I said.

She told me. Now her eyes focused on me. She was being frank and brisk about it.

What ? I said. I laughed. I suppose it was a shock.

She looked at me. I knew I had no rights to opinions in things like this anymore.

Sorry, I said. It's just I didn't think he was your type. I would have thought he was a little, you know, old for you ?

What's age got to do with anything ? she said.

I don't know, I said. I really don't.

I got out of the chair and wandered into the other half of the room. I stood looking out at the rough hole she'd made in the stone wall. It was like the one Desperate Dan used to punch people through. I'd seen all the mess and rubble in a pile outside. Now the floorboards under it were swept clean, except for a few bits of whitish mortar which must have kept crumbling and dropping out of it. I wandered back.

Perhaps I might have that drink now, I said.

Kitty was stood looking along the shelf of records and tapes. There's white wine, she said. Or there might be some brandy. Then again, there might not.

Wine'll be fine, I said. I didn't need to hear who did or didn't have the last of the brandy.

You know where the fridge is, she said. Perhaps I'll have one too.

I knew where the fridge was. I knew where everything was. Every record sleeve and cassette she was looking at, every book on the bookshelves, every piece of furniture. The fleck of white paint on the handle of the door I'd painted, which I'd forgotten to wipe off.

I opened the door and went into the kitchen. I stood looking around. I knew where everything was. The dining chairs from the secondhand shop. The cups and plates with the green rim, upside down on the steel draining board. The flies stuck on the spiral of the flypaper. In its little tray above the sink, even the used tablet of yellow soap, with the dark crack in it, seemed to be the one it always was. My old Philips radio.

But on the hook behind the back door, a straw hat with a red ribbon that she's never tried on with a coy, embarrassed laugh for me. And when I opened the white fridge that said Hotpoint there were the remains of cauliflower cheese in a dish, an unstarted chock of red skinned Edam on the slotted wooden cheeseboard from which the wooden-handled pronged knife was still missing, a few cut stalks of greenish celery in a glass jar, half a tomato on a plate, the cut side down... the economical leftovers of meals I hadn't shared. That no one had shared.

But had someone shared the first half of the bottle of wine that lay on its side, the cork banged too far in again for me to pull out by hand ?

You think you know everything about your wife. You think you know her inside out. And inside out is how you think you're going to leave her, when she tells you to get out. Like, on the side of the stainless steel sink, those rubber gloves she'd done the washing up in and then pulled off, white outside now, and pink in. Like a drawn chicken, you think, with its insides pulled out on the table. That's how you'll leave her. Then you see the blood and tubes are yours.

I knew where the corkscrew was too. In the drawer by the sink with the second-best cutlery we'd had as a wedding present. Next to the drawer with the baking stuff, the pastry cutters and flour sieves and rolls of greaseproof paper and the old mechanical egg-beater that whirred.

I opened the door to the little back porch. My wellingtons were still there under the bench, old mud dry on them. The outside door to the garden was unlocked. I opened it and stood looking out. Blackness. Silence. Miles and miles of Brecon Beacons, all the way to Hay. I've always thought my wife must be very brave or very unimaginative to carry on living here on her own. I closed the door, locked it, and went back in.

I opened the wall-cupboard where the glasses were and took two out. I poured wine into both and went into the living room, taking the last inch in the bottle too. There was some Scott Joplin on. I gave Kitty her drink and sat down. Our eyes met that second before we drank, the way they do when two people have a drink. I raised the glass slightly, though there was nothing to toast. I tasted the wine. This would have to be my first and last glass. I lit another ciggy. Four.

Can I have another one of those ? Kitty said.

She'd just put one out. She had her hands open ready so I threw the packet of cigarettes, then the lighter one-handed. Kitty doesn't even catch the way women usually do. She took out a cigarette and lit it. Got it going, you could almost say. One arm folded, the cigarette held upright in front of her again, she looked across at me.

It didn't go all that successfully, she said. To be frank.

I didn't say anything. I was watching her smoke this unheard-of second cigarette. She studied the ash forming at the tip.

He was scared all the time, she said.

What of ?

Just if we went out anywhere, she said. Of being seen. Not that we did go out, much. She touched ash carefully on the rim of the saucer. I don't suppose it was scared, she said. I suppose it was guilty.

Oh, I said.

Well, not all the time, she said. But sometimes. Sometimes he'd just go missing. You know ?

Go missing ? I said.

Absent, she said. Distant. Out to lunch. The sudden quietness. The haggard stare. The worried fingernail. A woman can tell these things. She laughed. The hard, sure laugh that was anything but. Even when he came here, she said. Well, she said, that's mostly what we did. He came here.

To this house. My house. I thought of the room up there. The brass bed in it and the afternoon light. My bed. And the rug in front of the fireplace. The sofa she was sitting on. The kitchen table he had touched her at. The walls he had backed her against. This house where I knew where everything was. Where everything had been.

We sat there for a while. So, I said. What's the position ?

With what ? she said.

You know what I mean, I said. At the moment. You and him.

She blew cigarette smoke out in a long, unpracticed stream. What always happens ? His wife found out. I don't know how. I had one last, furtive phone call from him crying off one of our afternoons. I haven't seen him since.

Oh, I said.

It was all right for a while, she said. For what it was. But it was never going to be any good. If you know what I mean. I don't think he was really ready for it. For an affair.

But you were, you bitch, I thought. You were wet for one.

That's the word, isn't it ? she said.

I don't know what the word is, I told her.

The tape clicked off in the room, at the silent end of the spool. I hadn't even heard it playing.

I keep thinking I'm going to run into his wife, she said. But so far I haven't.

I looked at the light from the table lamp through the wine I'd hardly touched in the glass.

I quite like his wife, Hal, she said. I always have liked her. I suppose I liked them both. I know you didn't, much.

Anyway, she said. I suppose he's got to be extra careful these days. Now he's a Shadow bloody spokesman or whatever.

She gave a laugh of ludicrous and inappropriate gaiety. She got up and went to the machine, ejected the tape, turned it over and re-slotted it. Or have we heard this side already ? she said. She looked at me.

Don't ask me, I said.

She shrugged and pressed the button. She sat down. The other side started. So, she said. Now you've had it. All the dirt that's fit to print.

41

I looked at her. All the unhappiness and grief we cause each other, I thought. And cause ourselves.

And, most of all, cause me.

I looked at my watch. Got a long drive, I said. I think I'd better go.

I got to my feet. She did too.

I looked at her. Her eyes, just for that second, stirred darker blue, anxious. She put her hands on her hips and put her bare arms back slightly. I saw her brown shoulders, and the thin crease of her armpit under the hem of the pink singlet top; and that shadowed line that turns from pectoral to breast. Kitty never has believed in chance. She believes in muscle tone, and showing it.

I'll put it like this, she said. You don't have to.

Don't I ? I said.

Not if you don't want to, she said.

I looked at her, and her pupils went darker again. If I didn't go, I wondered how long we would carry this thing onwards with us, like a dead baby. Or something bitterer than that. More blameworthy. The way these things always are someone's fault, someone else's unknowable pleasure. The hatefulness there is in that. That there was now in this house. Where ? I wanted to ask her. Where exactly ? And how many times ?

If you stay, she said, get one thing clear. I'm not interested in a one-night stand.

I shrugged. I was pretty nonchalant about it all. I've had enough of those, I said.

Because it was the thing to say. But of course I hadn't. I hadn't had enough at all. Not by a long shot. That was the reason I was there.

Another View

NIA WILLIAMS

Nia Williams was born in Cardiff, educated at Rhydfelen, Exeter and Reading. She now lives somewhat reluctantly in Basingstoke, where she works as a freelance editor and feature writer. Her work has appeared in a range of Literary Magazines including Cambrensis.

I am hanging upside down in my own car. My throat pulling hard, my head like a pressure cooker, and this is what has brought me back to consciousness. My eyes are already open, framing the view without judgement. Sky is like a winter sea. Trees droop towards it. My shoulder crackles in pain: the seat belt, straining under my weight. Can't place my arms and legs just yet. Strange click-clicking sound outside, and birdsong. My first sculpted thought is about my glasses, where are they ? Then I remember, and I think: 'Lucky I wore my contact lenses today.'

When I was ten I thought everyone had one bad eye and one useful eye. I thought it was part of the human condition, one functioning, the other for symmetry's sake. Like the idiot left hand and the hard-working right. My father would fill the living room doorway and rumble to my mother: 'She's too near that damn TV again,' but I thought he just didn't like me watching. He never complained that I was too near my schoolbooks. Gareth Trevor said to me in the Maths class once, 'Why do you scrunch your eyes up all the time ?' To me that was like asking 'Why does your heart beat ?' It was just part of the way life was, like coming to school, like supper at six, like my father's imploded anger and my humiliated squint and blush. Gareth Trevor was quite a gentle boy, then. We used to sit together in the cloakroom at dinnertime, hidden among the moist hangings, white sandwich boxes balanced on our knees. We would peer through the milky plastic at the folds of our sandwiches and guess as we peeled off the lids: 'Cheese and pickle ?' 'Smells like corned beef to me.' One morning, Gareth Trevor and I sat on a desk in an empty classroom during break, and I told him about my nightmare, of a girl stuffed into a well, up to the lips in filthy water, not screaming or struggling, just finished, and nobody remembering she was there. We sat in silence for a while, locked together by fear. Of what ? Something vicious and permanent, just over the horizon, outside the school walls, beyond this room. Then he said, 'Let's write a contract. In case we ever get trapped or stranded, and we'll promise to remember about each other.'

'We hereby faithfully swear,' we wrote, in a spare exercise book, 'always to remember, even when everyone else forgets and even if we lose everything.' We sat there, shoulders touching, curved over our contract, blanketed from the playground yelps and mews. They were the happiest twenty minutes of my life.

My right hand makes itself known, prickling with tiny electric shocks. It's hanging below my head, almost touching the car roof. Some distant memory of hospital dramas prompts me to move my fingers and to conclude that nothing is broken. Still can't locate my legs, but the left arm is beginning to register its existence, folded and tucked up under, or rather over my chin. On the telly cars generally explode quite soon after turning upside down. Tell myself to try and get out, get clear, but the words are cool and scripted and my body takes no interest. I think of my father, sitting up in his hospital bed, plumped up, taking charge, ordering tea and attention. I think of his wide, fleshy cheeks, black-red with years of fury and drink. Maybe I could say I was driving too fast. He'd like that. He wouldn't believe it though. Maybe he doesn't need to know about this.

He found our contract a week after we wrote it. It fell out of my Maths book as I scrabbled through my homework one evening. He picked it up slowly and read it to my mother, dropping each word with care into her silent lap. '"Even if we lose everything,"' he read, and paused, looking at my mother, not at me. '"Even if we lose everything." Says it all, doesn't it.' Then he closed it in one hand and dropped the cabbaged paper on to my book. 'Says it all.'

My father liked winners. One of my earliest memories is of crying over the dog's last puppy, the runt, splayed on the basket floor like a damp flannel, panting its first and last breaths. 'Come on now, girl,' said my dad, giving my arm a twitch, 'Don't waste your tears. He's finished. Not fit for life.' There was a certain path, a track through the maze, that's how he saw it; and it was up to every one of us to shove aside distractions and head for the light.

By the end of my second year in school we were being sent home with lists of subjects and career choices. I wanted to do Welsh. I had this fantasy about talking fluent length with my Nan, when we visited her damp house in Llanelli, baffling my parents, dodging my father's commentary and footnotes. I imagined being a new person, with a set of shining plans and thoughts to go with my new words. I mumbled a suggestion to my mother, handing her the third year timetables. I thought from the tilt in her eye that she favoured the idea. My father, home from work, snapped up the list and barked at it: 'Welsh ? Welsh ? What in God's name do you think they're about in that place ? What are they teaching this child ? How to crouch in a corner for the rest of her days ? How to lock herself away from the rest of the world ?'

Even now I can't bring myself to take an evening class in the language. I suppose I've accepted that he was right.

I wonder why I'm so sleepy. Harnessed the wrong way up in a car in a ditch, probably about to be blown to smithereens, and I'm having trouble staying awake. Maybe it's shock. Maybe it's that thick smell of petrol settling around my throat. Suddenly my foot dislodges itself and my knee shoots up against my left arm and chin, clamping my tongue between my teeth. Flash of pain, soothed by the sweet taste of blood.

Funny really, that I'm so cool about all this. I was always so emotional, so open to the elements, my mother would say. Such a loser.

When we went back to school for the third year Gareth Trevor had learned how to win. He had a sneer, a sense of irony and a gang of male butties and could no longer be seen to endure my presence. There seemed to have been some conspiracy during the long summer holiday; everyone had decided to start growing up. Other girls in my form had discovered periods and lip salve, and we were developing an acid look to repel all enemies. I had to be friends with Ceri Treaves, who wrote 'Jesus is my Friend' in big round letters on her satchel, and was another spare. We sat in the front row, so that I could see the blackboard, and rounded off the numbers. Strangely enough my father approved of Ceri Treaves. Maybe because she was entirely confident in her world: prayer, faith, righteousness. She missed the boys phase, the giggling phase, the staring horrified into the mirror for hours on end phase. She just carried on from year to year, with her pale, oval face and her steady eyes and her hard little pebble-breasts, never needing to grow from childhood because she'd never really been a child. She went to Oxford, became a lecturer, I think, and my father still mentions her from time to time: there was a clever girl. There was a girl who knew what was what.

For pity's sake, Ceri Treaves is hardly the issue now. She's probably gliding through the Oxford streets to her calm home, while I'm dangling like a puppet in a wrecked car. That reek of petrol is seeping behind my eyes and down my throat and the sky is swelling with an early sunset. My contact lenses are beginning to burn. I might blow up any second and would anyone know ? My father is the only member of my family left, and who would tell him ? Who would know he was anything to do with me ?

My Nan's legs were fascinating. Too intimate: I was embarrassed by the spread and settle as she sat down, before she gave her skirt a token snap, failing every time to cover her petticoat. I would sit by the black-tile fire in her kitchen, petting Llew, the spaniel, and try not to stare at the sinister gloom beyond her knees. I had a nervous habit of clutching the sides of my dress and had nightmares about forgetting to wear it to school. Nan was shockingly casual about her own body, despite Dad's accusing 'Mother,' when she hoisted up her clothes to step onto a chair and reach the gravy boat from her dresser. 'Twt, lol, David,' she said, 'there's nothing new to see there.' He always called her Mother, always, as if to explain why he still entered her world. Except once, now that I think of it, when they called to say she'd been found pissing on the front flower beds. I heard my mother as she passed him the phone, muttering urgently, relieving herself was the term she used, and I tightened with fear of Nan's strangeness and my father's temper. He wasn't cross, though. He said 'Put her on to me, please Mrs Davies,' and he sounded firm and sensible, like a nurse. Then his voice rose a little. 'Oh, Mam,' he said. 'Oh, Mam.'

I can remember that now. I can remember how he sounded, not like a father at all. And here I am, in the creeping dark, staring at my own flesh, that dips and gathers and grows cold, slap in the middle of my nightmare, showing my all to the black trees, twt lol, nothing new there. Wasting my time and energy, digging into memories, excavating fragments of people I never really knew. My parents never told me a single recollection of their own. I didn't even know my mother's age and hardly noticed when her weak brown hair died into white. All I gathered about my father's youth was passed to me by Nan. 'He always wanted out,' she would say, adding oddly, 'and good for him.' To me the warmth and cake-smell of my Nan's little house was a haven, a release from our symmetrical rooms, where the furniture was backed along the walls. But she wanted him out too. She never spoke to him in her own language. He was pushed across the gulf from the start and pointed in the direction of the world. But he never got out, did he. Stuck in the no-man's land between home and future, angry, thrashing around. Ceri Treaves had followed her path, broken out, and I just made do, stayed put, cowered in my corner.

This afternoon he sat up in his bed and told me I had no thrust in me. 'Still mincing about in that nothing job, trundling around in that shopper's car. Get out there, show what you're made of, get shot of this place, see the world.' He started his aggressive cough, spitting onto the blanket. 'In God's name, child, do something with your life while you still have one.' Ranting and dribbling, pulling and turning against the confines of his crisp sheets. I nodded, as usual, shrugged, as usual, wiped his chin, kissed his forehead.

Towards the end Nan was hoarding things: newspapers, food, milk bottles. She became a fortress-builder, stacking her Daily Mirrors and Women's Weeklies into solid walls, leaving herself a narrow corridor from kitchen to front door. I went there with my parents after she'd gone to the home, to collect some things and meet a man from Social Services. There was an alien stench now, still warm, but sour and musty. I stood at the front door and watched my mother and father step gingerly over old chop bones, brushing from side to side of the rustling battlements. I heard my father growling, 'She'd have walled herself in completely, if we'd let her.'

The pain in my shoulder is fading. Is it numb, or am I losing consciousness ? I can still feel the tug of my hips, though, as my legs strain to touch ground again. Hand is wet, hot against my face, comforting. Someone will come soon, maybe in time. It'll be a stranger, and I'll be covered up in a soft, red blanket and taken to a safe place. I'm trying to imagine them telling my father, his reaction. A whip of anger, an avalanche of coughing, or maybe not. He might be quite still, sitting quietly, and then he might say in a different, a smaller voice, 'Oh, in God's name, child. In God's name.' I try to compare the two voices; I struggle to know which is real. But the darkness and this damn petrol are too strong, pressing on my tired mind. Maybe I should let them win, now. Maybe it's best if nobody knows I'm here.

The Perfumed Garden

GEE WILLIAMS

Gee Williams was born in Saltney, Clwyd. She was educated at Hawarden Grammar and Culham College, Oxford. She is a lecturer in English at Wirral Metropolitan College where she also runs the Writer's Workshop. She is married to a physicist.

I t was the best and worst thing that had happened to either.

Her voice was a thick, rich, warm colour. It came languidly through the air to him, flowing across his face and soaking into his scalp.

'I'm sorry ?'

'I said what a beautiful animal. Your dog, I mean.'

There was a hint of uncertainty, just at the last, which cooled the consonants. Yet the voice was no less appealing.

'Yes, she is beautiful, or so I'm told.' he said.

He heard and felt sharp exultation. 'Oh, oh.. I'm ...oh, what a stupid thing to say. I didn't think.'

'No. No.' Instantly he regretted the reflex jibe. 'It's, er. it's my fault. Really.' He cast his eyes down because he'd found out that that was what normal people did in contrition. 'You, I mean I, felt at a disadvantage, you see. Get the joke ? So I suppose I tried to turn the tables. Bad habit.'

There were a few terrifying seconds of silence. His punishment if only she'd known it.

'Of course.' she said. 'It's only natural, and it was a stupid thing for me to say, and it is a very beautiful dog.'

There was no way of telling if she was about to walk off, or had begun to walk off for that matter. He had to think quickly.

'Would you do something for me ?' he blurted out. 'Before you go... would you... I mean have you got the time... would you describe her for me ?'

'Describe the dog ?'

'Yes, if you don't mind. I've only had her for a few months. I had another before of course, but she died.'

'But you must know what she, you must know what she's like ?' she protested.

'I know she's a white Alsation, German Shepherd or whatever. But I can't imagine what that's like. No picture, no memory, nothing. You seem to be interested in dogs and, and...' He knew he was going on for too long, should pause in case she wanted to speak. But he daren't, 'and I've found you get the best descriptions from people who know about, care about, what they're seeing.'

He forced himself to stop.

'I'd be glad to,' said the voice, washing over him like a wave of lava, and a hand was laid on his free arm, so that it seemed he and the dog conducted her to the seat.

He'd thought the garden scented until she sat beside him. Then the aromatic herbs and flowers, each with its braille name plaque, gave way to shampoo, soap, and, and, toothpaste, that was it, spearmint toothpaste.

'Did you know this was a garden planted for the blind ?'

She gave a laugh, half-apologetic, half-wicked. 'I did. I'm afraid I read the notice.'

'Of course.'

'How long have you been... ?' almost he could hear her search for a synonym, a euphemism, a politically correct terminology for life lived in the dark.

'How long have I been blind ? Twenty years. Since I was three.'

'Do you remember colours ?' she asked gently.

'Yes, I do.'

'Right, I'll start with the colour,'she added briskly. 'Your dog, she's a most unusual colour for a G.S.D. Pale cream, or milky white, depending on your point of view. A girl with that colour hair we'd call a platinum blonde.'

He felt her bend and lean across to the dog. Presumably she was running its platinum blond hair through her fingers. 'Most German Shepherds are black and tan: black body, head and tail and tan legs.'

'I've always imagined tan to be orange, like a tangerine.'

'Well not quite. More brown than orange, really. More earth than sun, if you get my meaning.'

'I do.'

'But your dog, well she's quite a beauty. Pale coat.' She paused, obviously scrutinising her subject. 'And those eyes, they're pale too. Almost gold. Kind, as well. Dogs have a way of looking at you, it's always one thing or the other. Either they've never been hurt or let down and they're kind, or they've been knocked about, beaten you know... something like that, and they look at you. Well it's as though they wouldn't believe what you said, not if it came with a signed certificate from the Pope.'

He laughed. 'From the Pope ?'

'Oh, dear,' she said. 'You're not a Catholic are you ?'

'No.'

'Thank goodness.'

He expected her to elaborate but she didn't. All he had was the warm air that surrounded her body flowing into the space between her and his bare arm.

'Do I look like a Catholic ? he said nervously.

Her laugh was low and thrilling. 'More Scots Presbyterian, I'd say.'

'But I'm Welsh,' he protested.

'So am I. From Aberystwyth... and you ?'

'Born in Bangor.'

'Ah, well,' she said, 'that's Chester for you. An English city with hardly any English in it.'

He tried to keep the urgency from his voice when he asked

his next question. 'Do you live here now ?' but she had caught it and her reply came kindly but firm. 'I'm afraid not. I'm, I'm just visiting, just for a couple of days. I'm staying over there,' she nodded, despite the pointlessness of the gesture, 'in Bath Street.' Would he know ? Had he been told of the terrace of red brick, Victorian houses running up from the Dee ? 'They've only a little yard behind them, so I came along the river for a breath of fresh air.'

'And into this garden,' he said. 'I'm glad to say.'

'Oh,' was all that came back.

There was never a time he'd resented his blindness more. 'Are you, look, I've got to ask, are you blushing ?'

'Yes. I am,' and without a word he felt his hand taken and turned and the very tips of his fingers tapped against her burning cheek.

'Thank you.'

'You're welcome,' she said.

'Do you know one of the worst things, about not being able to see ? Well apart from the obvious. It's not being able to touch. I think you have to see when to do it, when you can put your arm around someone's shoulders or pat a child on the head or, or hold a hand.'

If it was a hint she didn't take it, nor his hand again, instead murmuring, 'I'd never thought of that.'

The dog chose the moment to fling itself down beneath the seat, sighing theatrically.

'What's she called ?'

'Jenny.'

'She's quite an actress. You should have called her Sarah.'

'What do you mean ?'

'After Sarah Bernhart,'

'Oh, right, yes,' he said rather too quickly.

'And it's my name too.'

'Is it ?' He felt delighted to be told. 'Sarah, yes you sound like a Sarah. Sarah. It's a lovely name.'

'My other one isn't. It's Pugh.'

He held out his hand although it was awkward to do so, side by side. This time she did take it and saw her own pumped vigorously up and down in the way that a child apes the adult ritual. 'Nice to meet you, Sarah. I'm John Brookes.'

'It's nice to meet you, John.'

'You have very slim fingers.'

'Er, yes I suppose I do.'

'Are you small ? No, let me tell you. You're about,' he took a measure by tapping his own chest with the heel of his hand, 'five foot four with blue eyes and dark hair.'

Her hesitation made him fear he'd overstepped the mark and he swore inwardly. How could he gauge the level of familiarity and get it right with so little to go on ? But when she answered, nothing too terrible seemed to have come of it.

'Well, the eyes are right. Blue-grey, anyway, but you've added a couple of inches. I'm five-two.'

'And the hair ?'

'Not so dark.'

'O.K.'

He sat back and closed his own useless blue eyes so that she could see him conjure up her picture in his mind: thin but brilliant with a rose-pink glow coming off her skin. It was the shade of a piece of precious glass his mother had owned, still owned, in fact. It was his strongest, best-held colour. It meant perfect happiness. But to be the centre of so much attention seemed to unnerve rather than flatter. He felt her small movements at his side and guessed at discomfort.

'The, the dog,' he prompted.

'Oh, yes, the dog. Well, she's very big, even for a large breed. She's a great, pale wolf of a dog, and I think she'd like to walk.'

'How do you know ?'

She laughed again. 'She's giving me an 'every dog will have his day' look. Am I spoiling hers do you think ?'

'Well, we don't usually sit. No point. Once around the pond, then back over the bridge, that's our day.' He hated the words even as they left his lips. They sounded pathetic, self-pitying, all those things that repelled him in others, often other blind, and it was unjust, because they were not him, or at least, not the him he was most of the time. 'The afternoons,' he said firmly, 'are pretty busy.'

'Then we'd better get going or you'll be running late.'

He caught the hint of mockery and could have kissed for it. Not many people dared make fun.

Fast and seemingly super-confident, he strode out towards the centre of the park, the dog's harness in one hand and her arm in the other. Really, he knew he was just showing off. A couple speaking French they overtook and left their voices dwindling to a few nasal aspirants on the breeze. Voices of a Japanese group faded quickly past.

'You're right,' he said. 'Chester's an English city with no English in it.'

'Er, yes.'

To his surprise he realised she was out of breath.

'I'm sorry, I'm going too fast.'

'It's all right,' she gasped but they slowed down, nonetheless. A tremor entered the voice even as it stoutly proclaimed there was nothing wrong. This and her lightness of touch, and the memory of her smallness on the seat beside him came together and produced a new image: one of frailty, of sickness even. The rose-coloured glow dimmed.

As if on cue, she coughed. Then, like a harbinger of numerous black imaginings, the plangent call of an ambulance overwhelmed and obliterated the entire world. All he could do was wait for it to butt a path through the city's traffic and fade away to the north, which was the opposite direction to the sun's warmth on the back of his head.

'Loud noises must be a problem,' she said. 'Mind you, your dog never flinched.'

'She's well trained and yes, they are. Like putting the lights out for someone sighted perhaps... sudden lack of info.'

'Like silence?'

'No, much worse. There's no such thing as silence anyway. The quieter it is, the more you can hear... and, look, are you O.K. ?'

'Fine, just a cough, that's all.'

'But you don't smoke,' he couldn't help pointing out.

'Ah, there's clever.'

'Not really, I'll bet even the sighted can smell a smoker.'

She chuckled. It was deep and thrilling. 'Even the sighted can smell a smoker,' she mimicked. 'Now I'd call that a sightist remark.'

'Sightist ?'

'You know, like chauvinist and racist and sexist.'

'And ageist ?'

'And ageist,' she agreed. 'Let's walk on, shall we ?'

Ahead of them a goose honked belligerently and he felt the dog stiffen although it maintained its slow pace. With a shock he realised they were nearer the pond than he'd calculated, that he'd been relying on his companion instead of meting out his own mental map as he moved through the unseen spaces.

'Is there a goose on the path ?' he asked. I don't want Jenny to scare it.'

'No, it's not a goose, it's a gander, and they're both inside the railings around the edge of the pond. It's not the dog, I don't think.' She had to raise her voice over the sonic missiles of malice being blasted towards them. 'It's having a go at everything and everybody. It's got a mate on a nest in the reeds.'

'Oh, then we shouldn't come between man and wife. Shall we turn back ?'

On the downward path returning them to the river he could catch the sound of her breath coming easily and softly now and his recent fears that had turned her into an ailing, Bohemian Mimi seemed ridiculous... ridiculous but also revealing. It revealed how much he cared. Soon they would be at the double gates that closed off the Groves from the cobbled lane leading to the suspension bridge, and his home across the Dee. But where he turned left she would turn to the opposite direction and his throat tightened with a sudden longing to keep her with him, not to let her walk off into the darkness where that vibrant voice and light step would be swiftly overlaid by background noise.

'Sarah ?' he said.

'Yes John.'

It was only the second time they had spoken each other's names.

'Sarah, this may seem like a strange question, coming from a blind man, but...'

'But ?'

'But do you believe in love at first sight ?'

He couldn't bear it. As soon as the words were out, he couldn't bear the thought of his response. This was the horror of blindness, of the blind boy and the blind teenager and the blind man always surrounded by kind and solicitous, never taking the sneers and rebuffs, never toughening up for when it would really matter. He burst into laughter to hide the misery of waiting and was relieved to hear her join in.

'Love at first sight,' she laughed and then, seriously, 'Yes,

I do believe in it, for some at least.'

'Oh God,' he whispered, 'Is there anyone near ?'

'No, but.'

'Sarah.' Her arm was still in his. It was the easiest thing in the world to bend and bury his face in her fine, clean smelling hair and kiss her head, but she was away from him in an instant. He was left with the dog's harness resting in one hand and the knowledge that she was still very close, but out of reach.

'Sarah, I'm sorry. Please don't go. I didn't mean to upset you. I'm sorry.' His fear left him uncertain which way to direct his plea. 'I think I love you. That's what it is. I just didn't want you to walk away. I'm sorry.'

'No,' she said very quietly. 'I'm sorry. You haven't upset me, not at all. How could you ? But, oh, John, if I told you what I felt, it would only make things worse. Good-bye, my dear.' His hand was pressed by thin, cool fingers and then she was gone.

'Sarah, please wait.' But he knew she didn't hear him. The voices of strangers came between him and her retreating figure.

Since a blind man cannot chase a girl into a city, he stood still and the dog lay at his feet. After a while it occurred to him they may be blocking the path and he and Jenny retraced their route and sat amongst the lavender and santolina in what his mother, in her innocence, always called the Perfumed Garden.

Surrounded by the too familiar sounds and smells it was almost as though Sarah had never existed, but up Souters Lane and along Vicars Lane and into Bath Street a small neat woman in her sixties pushed feebly through the tourist crowds, and the tears streamed down her face.

Antifreeze

T.J.DAVIES

T.J.Davies was born in Banbury, Oxford. He was educated at St. David's College, Lampeter and King's College, London. His writing has appeared in Planet, Radical Wales and Cambrensis.

I always knew Brundell was dangerous. A loose cannon, unpredictable. It's not that I mind Specials as such. They come in all shapes and sizes, and God knows we need them, with regular Police levels being what they are. But Brundell had a hidden agenda. You could tell from the splinter-short hair, the thrust of the jaw, the glint in the eye, what kind of copper he'd make if his application to join the regular Force was successful. I'd seen his sort before. No interest in the reality of proper policing, the door-to-door enquiries, the mountains of paperwork, the road safety sessions in school playgrounds. None of that was dramatic enough for him. What he wanted was trouble, someone to make his day.

Just the sort you can do without.

We were parked, he and I, in a lay-by on the A470 South of Merthyr. As usual, cars came towards us at ferocious speed, then slowed desperately as the drivers spotted us, lying in wait like a leopard on a branch. Brundell was sounding off about his favourite subject, the violence of modern society and his role in it. I sighed inwardly. For all his mouth and trousers, for all the hours he spent in the gym and on the dojo, I'd yet to see him in action. Every shift with him had been quiet. And I'd worked with him a lot, more than anyone else. Someone in personnel must have a grudge against me. I looked at my watch. Only half an hour gone, seven and a half to go. Like being stuck in a lift with a Millwall supporter.

'I don't scare easy,' he said eventually, concluding some

rambling observation about how good he was in a tight spot.

'Oh, I do, I scare awful easy,' I replied, daring him to believe me.

Just then the radio crackled into life and off we went.

Trefynydd is a long string of a town with a wilderness beyond both ends. An old mining town which, like all the other towns of the valleys, didn't have any mining left, or much of anything else. Most of the shops and pubs had closed, and were boarded up with plywood covered in flyposters and graffiti. Rubbish blew along the unswept streets, and people hung about with the air of not having anything else to do. It didn't look like the kind of place to come if you wanted cheering up.

We turned slowly into the High Street and moved slowly along, light flashing, siren off, looking for signs of trouble. At first nothing seemed to be wrong, but then after a few moments I began to pick up the signs that something wasn't right. Men and women stood about, clustered unnaturally around bus-stops and in doorways, the human fall-out of an incident in progress. They were gossiping hotly and looking repeatedly up the road to some unseen site of disturbance, as if at the place where a whirlwind had just passed.

Then we saw him.

I stopped the car and we both sat still for a moment, looking.

'Christ. Big, isn't he ?' said Brundell.

'He's not small,' I replied, happy for once to agree with him.

He had come lurching out of an alley and stood swaying unsteadily in the middle of the street like a pantomime drunk. He was waving a bottle about and seemed to be addressing comments to the world at large, and as he did so the knots of people seemed to shrink away from him, leaving him in a pool of emptiness. I nudged the car closer and stopped again. He was what people used to call unkempt. Tousled red hair, a scrub of stubble, scruffy jeans and a shirt with some of the buttons missing.

And big. Very, very big.

'Right, we can't sit here all day, ' I said, opening the door. 'Let's go and see what's what.'

'What're we going to do, cuff him ?' asked Brundell.

'Dunno yet,' I said, getting out of the car. I didn't much fancy trying to put handcuffs on a grizzly bear. But maybe it wouldn't come to that.

We walked sedately towards him, and I tried to size things up as we went. For all our flashing lights and uniforms he didn't seem to have noticed us yet, and was continuing his oration to anyone who cared to listen. We stopped for a moment, a mutual, unspoken decision, an island of calm before the possible storm. I looked at Brundell and frowned. Far from composing himself, he was getting stoked up for trouble. He was shifting his shoulders about like a man squaring up for a fight, and his mouth had assumed the sort of worm-shape that skinheads get when they ask someone what they're looking at.

'Look don't try any fancy stuff, all right ? Let me handle this, and just back me up if I need it,' I said. He glanced at me but said an unknowable nothing. We moved on, past the cowering bands of spectators.

'He've just shot a brick through the Co-op window,' called a woman from the pavement.

'O.K. love, we'll sort it out after, ' I replied as we drew up to him. Only then did he seem to notice us.

'Come and join the party boys,' he said in a husky valleys accent, waving the bottle towards us. His eyes were unfocused and dilated, and I wondered if I could talk him down with no trouble. The next few seconds would be crucial. In my experience, if someone is going to cut up rough, they'll do it straight away or not at all.

'Now now lovely boy,' I said in a soft tone. 'Why don't you just come along with us? You've had a bit of fun from the look of it. Perhaps it's time to settle down and sober up a bit.' I braced myself as he looked from me to Brundell and back again.

'Noh, the party's just starting, boys, come and have a drink,' he said, offering the bottle again. I looked at it, a dumpy black plastic thing.

'Not just now, lovely boy,' I said, 'What's your name anyway ? I can't keep calling you lovely boy, you'll be getting the wrong idea.'

'Ah, Malc, my name is, Malcolm Evans, but everyone do call me Malc,' he said, swaying a bit.

'O.K. Malc, now why don't you tell us what that is you've been drinking. It doesn't look like booze to me,' I said. Out of the corner of my eye I could see Brundell moving off to the side.

'This ? Antifreeze. Good drop of stuff,' he said.

I edged towards him.

'Antifreeze ? What you drinking that for ?' I asked.

'It's all I got left in the house; I finished all the booze, even the cooking sherry,' he said, tottering to the side. I put a hand out to steady him and carefully cupped his elbow in my hand.

'Now now, you can do yourself a lot of harm drinking that stuff, Malc. Why don't you come back with us and let the doctor check you over ?' I said.

He tried to focus on me. I held my breath.

'Well,' he said at length, dropping his gaze and looking still and thoughtful. I almost had him where I wanted him. 'Come on, now,' I said quietly, drawing him towards me by the elbow.

Just then Brundell jumped him.

It was all over in seconds. After a brief scuffle, Malc had me by the wrist at arms length, and Brundell by the neck, head trapped under the crook of his elbow, like a medieval ghost. Malc turned in a slow circle, as if wondering what to do with us. I glanced at the groups of people watching us, and felt myself go red. For a moment I held the gaze of a middle-aged woman with a shopping bag. She stepped forward into the road.

'D'you want us to call the Police ? she asked me.

'Er, no it's alright for now love. I'll keep you posted,' I said.

'O.K. then,' she replied, stepping back.

I didn't quite know what I was going to do, but I still felt I could get round Malc without too much trouble, provided nothing else went wrong. For all the fact that he was technically resisting arrest by now, I reckoned that he was less interested in fighting us than he was in stopping us fighting him, and that if it hadn't been for Brundell's stupid behaviour we'd have all been driving down to Merthyr by now.

'Now look, Malc, you know you can't go on like this, you'll be getting into serious trouble,' I said. As I talked I tried to peel his fingers off my wrists, but he had a grip like a Scotsman on a five pound note, and I couldn't shift even one of them.

'Get him back to the car,' said Brundell from under Malc's armpit.

'Up to the car, is it ? O.K. boys,' said Malc, turning us all around and heading back the way we had come. As he led us along like a couple of recalcitrant children, I carried on talking.

'O.K. Malc, why don't you tell us what's brought this on ? I bet you're a tidy sort of a boy most of the time, something must have happened to start all this off. Why don't you tell us about it, before something really bad happens ?' I said. He laughed as we moved along.

'Aye you could say something have brought it on all right. Ever seen a brick wall being knocked down ? I used to think life was a bit like a wall being built. You know, you finishes school, that's a couple of rows, then you gets a job, that's another couple of rows, then you gets married and has a family, and you goes on like that 'til you got your wall in front of you, all finished and strong. But up here it's like they've come around and knocked all the walls down. First they closed the pits and took all the jobs, now the missus have run off and taken the kids, and now today they wants to repossess the house. It's like all I got left now is a pile of dust and rubble, and somehow it don't seem enough,' he said. We had nearly reached the car.

'We're all of us skittles in the bowling alley of life Malc,' was all I could think of to say.

'Here we are boys,' said Malc, 'I'll drive.'

My career began to melt away in front of my eyes. What would the headlines be like ? I shook my head, and wondered what to do next.

Just then Malc's grip on my wrist slackened, then dropped away altogether. Brundell's head disappeared from under his arm as he stood red-faced and upright. Malc had gone very still and silent, and seemed to be physically shrinking as he stared at the white bonnet in front of him.

'I'm going to be sick,' he whispered. Before we could do anything, a jet of brown liquid squirted over the bonnet, spread out and ran off like an April shower.

'Dirty bastard,' said Brundell. I stood considering the situation. Malc looked as if he'd be putty in our hands now, but did I dare him to get in the car yet, in case he was sick again? Then a hissing sound from the bonnet drew my attention.

It was steaming languorously from the vomit, as you'd expect, but something else was happening as well. The amount of steam was increasing, and seemed to be turning into smoke.

Small bubbles of paint were beginning to appear all over the affected area. They swelled, linked up into irregular blobs and then popped and wrinkled away amid the waving fronds of smoke. Eventually the afflicted patch of paint contracted in on itself, splitting off from the surrounding area and slithering with a hiss down the slope of the bonnet until it fell in a crumpled heap onto the road. I looked at the naked grey metal of the exposed bonnet, framed by a crinkled brown fringe and as clear as the day it was pressed.

On the way back I radio'd ahead for the doctor to be ready, all the time keeping a close eye on Malc in the mirror. Brundell stared silently at the grey patch in front of him. Before long Malc uttered the words I had been dreading.

'I'm going to be sick again.'

I pulled over into a gateway not far short of where the road rejoined the A470. Malc stumbled out and started throwing up in a ditch. I prepared to wait for a while, but suddenly Brundell swore and jumped out after him. I jumped out after the pair of them, but by the time I got to them Brundell was beating the daylights out of Malc. I pulled him off and shoved him towards the car.

'Get back over there,' I shouted, turning to Malc.

'Bloody soft you are,' said Brundell as he went.

'Just get in and shut up,' I shouted as I helped Malc up. One eye was puffing up, his lip was split and his nose was bleeding. He trembled slightly as I led him back to the car.

I didn't trust myself to speak to Brundell on the way back. Towns like Trefynydd were full of Malcs waiting to happen, men brought up to face a life of hard work in dirty jobs that few people understood and fewer still would do. Face them with an eternity of nothingness and some of them were bound to go ballistic. But I wasn't going to try and explain that to Brundell. He'd have just called me a Social Worker.

Once we got back I handed Malc over to the doctor and went off to make my report and grab a coffee. My route took me past the duty Inspector's room, and as I approached it I could see that the door was open. I tried to hurry past, but the Inspector, who I believe held me in no high regard, spotted me and called out.

'Azzopardi, come in here for a minute will you.' he said. Reluctantly I stopped and went in, standing just inside the open door as if the distance from his desk would help soften the blows to come. For all that I'd managed to avoid being kidnapped in my own car, there was still the bonnet and the beating to be explained. Would I have to do so now, before I had time to collect my thoughts ? Would he raise again the time they stole the wheels off my car in lower Graig, and beat me over the head with it like a truncheon of my own stupidity ? My mouth was dry for coffee as I waited for him to speak.

He sat holding a piece of paper in each hand and looking from one to the other as if trying to decide which was best. Eventually he put them down and looked up at me.

'I've had a copy of Brundell's application to join the regular force sent down from headquarters, together with a request for a reference. I can't say I know him at all well, but I see from the duty sheets that you've worked with him more than anyone else. Perhaps you could give me some idea of what he's really like ?' he said.

'Certainly sir,' I said, turning and closing the door behind me.

The Sleepwalker and the Glazier

RACHEL PALMER

Rachel Palmer was born in Sussex. She has a life long interest in farming and during her teenage years spent as much time as possible on a Radnorshire sheep farm which gave her a lasting fascination for Welsh Agricultural History and Traditions. She qualified as a museum curator and learnt Welsh, in England after an inspiring period of training at the Welsh Folk Museum. She is married and lives and writes on a Radnorshire small-holding where she and her husband have raised and trained one of only a handful of pairs of draught oxen in Britain today.

There had been two crashes, the second one as some of the glass hit a little path below in the garden following the first echo of gunshot.

She stood completely still in front of the jagged window, her fists still raised high in front of her. Her eyes were open and she saw the first blood spiral down her forearm. There wasn't too much blood; not more than her rolled sleeve could absorb at her elbow. She was listening. It seemed impossible that none of the neighbours had heard the noise but there was no sound and no house lights were switched on. Without lowering her fists she rotated her arms slightly and examined the cuts without emotion. There were eight of them, five on her right hand and arm but the worst almost encircling her ring finger with a thick band of blood. She watched this as it swelled, and when the blood ring broke and sent a stream of blood down her arm with the rest, she moved. Stepping over the few spears of glass that had fallen inside the house she went into the bathroom and put her hands, one after the other, under the cold tap. While the water flowed over her hands she looked at her face in the mirror, fascinated by the emotionless mask that stared back. The water swept the blood away and under the flow all the cuts appeared very small and insignificant. There was only one piece of glass to remove. The blood surged again every time she withdrew a hand from the basin so she would have to get plasters on before she could sleep again. She was crashingly tired. By the time all the plasters were in place each was stained with blood but they seemed to hold the flow. She must remember not to tread on that glass on the carpet. She slept immediately.

Rain was forecast and the sleepwalker had a gaping hole in her bedroom window. She felt dulled with tiredness and the cuts on her arms were hurting for the first time. The broken glass and browning bloodstains on the window frame, washbasin, wall and bathroom floor looked like the remains of a late night party that had gone hideously wrong.

She washed her hair, picking off sodden sticking-plaster between the rinses and examining the stinging wounds. She dressed for work, disguising herself and her feelings in the costume of tailored efficiency. The fresh plasters on her hands were sufficiently numerous to suggest that there was a story to be told. She went to work but nobody asked for the story.

It was nearly five o'clock before the sleepwalker remembered that she had to find a glazier. It was cold and the rain had begun. The builder who answered the telephone had a slight speech impediment but was perfectly comprehensible and very helpful. She reassured him that it wasn't a double-glazed window, nothing complicated. Just a broken window requiring a single sheet of glass. She hadn't thought to measure it. She asked him to come and check the dimensions himself as she wasn't sure how much of the glass was concealed in the frame. He asked her how the window had got broken and she told him she'd been sleepwalking. He was obviously looking forward to meeting a sleepwalker.

He was one of those short, broad Valleys men whose massive miner's or farmer's arms looked absurd carrying a small pane of glass. This one had clearly had a lot of surgery on his face to correct a cleft palate and his hare lip accounted for his speech defect. She felt very warm towards him as one who had also undergone much private pain and bore the scars. His green eyes studied her unblinkingly while he carefully considered what to say first.

'I might have to order different glass.' He did not take his eyes off her face.

'Oh yes, I understand that.'

He was a man of few words which were released in small numbers at spaced intervals during their conversation. It was not until they had gone upstairs to see the broken bedroom window that he concluded his first remark.

'If it's not standard, see.'

The sleepwalker watched him as he measured the windowframe, seeing in his place a dark haired man who had sat beneath that window four months ago, wearing nothing but a striped shirt, helpless with laughter. She had been lying over the foot of the bed, naked, laughing with him until she felt almost sick. Then she crawled across to him and pushed her face into his shirt-front, feeling his body shaking with laughter and loving him, his soft warmth and for being the source of comfort and stimulation she had never known before.

'Lucky you didn't fall out.'

Neither of them had known on that September morning that she was expecting their baby. There was something wrong with her so she rarely menstruated and fertility drugs themselves induce symptoms of pregnancy. The miracle to her was that Gareth was there, whenever she wanted him, that he loved her so much and that he wasn't a shady, secret lover but a partner she could speak about and rely upon. That miracle was enough for her. She wasn't looking yet for a second one in a pregnancy against which the odds were so high.

'Have you done this before ?'

'What? Break a window sleepwalking or just sleepwalking?'

He thought about this.

'Sleepwalking.'

'Yes, just in the past few months.'

He had cried so desperately in this bedroom. She hadn't been able to sit up because of all the stitches in the great wound so he had leant over her so they could gently, carefully embrace. They had cried and cried together, at last having the privacy of her house for their grief after the brightly lit busy-ness of the hospital. She wondered now whether he had cried most for their daughter, for the shock of her own near death or for some other agony she did not understand. He had hung on to her and sobbed, 'I don't want to leave you,' in distorted gasps of grief over and over again, like a child exhausting itself in distress.

'You want to put a lock on that door, like. You could fall down the stairs.'

He had returned to London, his four days compassionate leave used up and he had never come back to Wales. When she had spoken to him on the telephone over the next month he had sounded so much like a stranger that she had actually asked him if he was being threatened. He had spoken as if a gun were being held to his head. He had laughed at the idea. He was not going to marry her and he did not want to see her again. Neither did he want any more of these painful telephone conversations.

The glazier hovered in the back doorway for over five minutes, urgently trawling his mind for further scraps of smalltalk before the sleepwalker was finally able to close the door on him. As soon as he was out of earshot she howled and howled like a dog.

Two nights later she was lying in the middle of her big bed, her back arched, her legs rigid, her arms drawn into her body so close that their muscles shuddered with tautness, her fists clenched so tightly that her fingernails made her palms bleed.

She had bitten her tongue and the insides of her cheeks in her nightmares and she could taste blood. Her nightclothes were sweaty and the dreams went on.

The sleepwalker stood up on the bed, moving slowly and staggering for a moment before she found her balance on the soft surface of the mattress. If only she had died with the baby then she would have never known the unbearable loss of the man and the infant. Her doctor had told her that anger would be better for her than grief but now at two-twenty in the morning it made no difference whether she yelped in misery or rage. Nobody heard.

She banged her forehead against the wall, wanting to break her head open to make people see the depth of her horrific distress; see how damaged she was by what had happened to her.

She got down off the bed and pulled one of the bedroom curtains aside. A streetlamp backlit the replacement windowpane and clearly showed the deep border of putty-covered fingerprints which the glazier had left as he eased the pane of glass into place.

She dressed in a pair of jeans and a sweater over her pyjama jacket and walked slowly into the back bedroom. She wished that she really was a sleepwalker and was not consciously having to address this determination to injure herself. It was not just self-hatred. Over the past months she had learnt to use shock and physical pain as the only way to control suicidal distress.

The glass from the back bedroom window made far more noise as all of it hit a hard surface, falling into the concrete yard below. She stood as before, fists raised, bleeding and waiting, already distracted from her grief by the blood and with listening for the first sound, inevitable, surely this time, of a neighbour.

She had to block off the cat-flap so that the two cats wouldn't follow her out and get splinters of glass in their paws. Outside, the yard was almost covered in jagged glass. She stood amongst it and it twinkled in the streetlight like a sparkling snow-scene in a cartoon film. David, apparently fully dressed, was at the gate.

'Elin, are you OK ?'

'I've done it again David. I've been sleepwalking again.'

He looked at her. The cool night air was soothing the tenseness of her hot face and as usual she turned to humour to protect herself.

'At this rate the glazier will be driving a BMW by Christmas.'

'Are you bleeding a lot ?'

'Yes. I'm going to hospital.'

'You can't go by yourself.'

'I have to do things by myself.'

She felt the increasing stickiness of the blood all over the steering wheel as she drove.

The male doctor and two female nurses on night duty were like a well rehearsed comedy act. It was strange for them to see a patient so bloodstained that she could have been the victim of an assassination attempt in little enough pain to immediately join their repartee. Elin was good material for their jokey atmosphere. She wondered at this power of shock to oust despair.

If she had been admitted that night to that same hospital as an attempted suicide she would have been forcibly mastered, isolated, questioned, observed and mistrusted. But she was safely a sleepwalker.

The doctor stitched her hand and three of her fingers. He then applied a thick anti-septic paste the colour of salad cream on top of the wounds.

'It looks like an Italian recipe,' she said.

They both laughed because it did. Bright red blood seeped from beneath the yellow cream all the way around and the stitches stuck out of the top. The effect was of a vanilla confection with strawberry sauce and some sort of surprise centre.

She laughed again, easily like a well-oiled party-goer. She was heady with the haven of the hospital, with the warm humour of its staff and that as a sleepwalker she was not condemned by the crime of the self-inflicted wound.

'Have you always been a sleepwalker ?' one of the nurses asked her.

'No. Only since I lost my baby.'

'Oh, how sad. I expect you are looking for it. You're lucky you woke up my love. I know of a sleepwalker who didn't and went back to bed all full of glass.'

She drove home, her injured fingers extended like bird's claws. She cleared up the glass as silently as she could. She was now very tired and quite calm. It was three thirty-five in the morning. She had two and a half hours' blessedly dreamless sleep.

The glazier correctly assumed that the back bedroom windows were of similar dimensions to the front ones. He replaced the glass while she was at work and called in for payment the following evening.

He was wearing his best clothes and he reached out and touched her shoulder as she turned away from him to get her chequebook. She turned back immediately and they both froze. His green eyes studied her and the hare lip contributed to an expression that was hopelessly sad.

Her hands shook a little when she wrote out the cheque. She thrust it at him and he almost ran from the house.

She stared at him unseeingly, wondering what choices were left now to her maimed soul at about three o'clock in the morning.

How '47 Saved the 'Chronic'

ROBERT MICHAEL SMITH

Robert Smith is thirty five years old and lives frugally in Beaufort. He teaches in Pontypool and claims to be Ebbw Vale R.F.C's most committed supporter.

My wife left one wet Monday in November, in search of a credit card more golden and capacious than mine.

The next day, I was slumped at my desk in the office of the Saffron Walden Weekly, doodling broken hearts and Buzzcocks lyrics on my note pad,when the proprietor strode in and announced imminent redundancies on a last in, first out basis. Guess who was last in ?

On the Wednesday I received a phone call from Aunty Blod back home in Blaencwm ; my mother had fallen down the stairs and snapped the head off her femur. According to Blod it was quite a neat break. Of course it would be neat ! My mother is South Wales' leading purveyor of neat. Cushions plump themselves in her presence. Minute specks of dust, caught in the sunlight which shuffles respectfully in through her snowblind nets, suspend themselves in mid-air rather than sully her sparkling sideboard.

I didn't go to work on Thursday and was sitting on the settee tippexing out my wife and her family from the wedding photos when the phone rang. It was a school friend. David Price-Edwards. With whom I had not conversed in ten years.

'You still in newspapers?' he asked, after the opening pleasantries were concluded. I saw myself, unshaven and methylated on a park bench, wrapped in a copy of the Sunday Times.

'I'm Chief Reporter with the Saffron Walden Weekly,' I

said, not adding that I was the only reporter.

'Dad's bought the Blaencwm Chronicle,' he told me.

'David,' I interrupted. 'Are you phoning to tell me that your father's been out to get a copy of the Chronic ?'

'No. He's bought the whole thing. He owns it. Fancy being Editor ?'

His offer came as such a shock that I'd accepted before it had registered.

In my retrospective justification, it all made perfect, practical sense. A move back to my roots at a time of emotional crisis. Being there for my mother when she left hospital. A chance to run my home town's weekly paper.

I moved into my mother's terraced house in time for her to come home for Christmas. I knew she was pleased because, although not one to parade her feelings, she'd let the nurses wrap tinsel around her zimmer frame.

Mr. Price-Edwards Senior had bought the Chronic from Miss Gwladys Benson, for thirty years its owner and editor. She had been all jam recipes and bouncing babies. He was bottom lines and sales projections.

'I want a paper of the people, by the people, for the people. I want human interest and political debate. I want local, national, international news. I want interviews, overviews, previews and reviews. But most of all. I want to shift ten k a week.'

Our current circulation was six thousand.

Sharon, the Chronicle's spiky-haired, gum-chewing Ace Reporter, was sprawled across the office's only comfortable chair.

'What's on today's agenda ?' I asked her.

'We're interviewing a woman in Brynteg about poltergeist activity.'

'Really ?'

'Yeh. Reckons her house is haunted by an old woman.'

'Flying crockery ? Pictures falling off the wall ? Unexplained noises ?'

'Nah. When they get up in the morning they find everything's been dusted and tidied away and strange messages written on the phone pad.'

'Like what ?'

'Like, "put your vest on, it's bitter out." And, "take a hanky, you never know." She reckons it's her nan.'

Bob, a jowly, bouncy forty bristling with photographic gear, labradored in and thrust a piece of paper at me.

'From Eddie,' he explained.

'Eddie ?'

'Eddie Roberts. Secretary of the rugby club. It's Saturday's match report.'

'Right,' I said. 'That Eddie. Well, you two go and see a woman about her spook and I'll take a glance at this.'

I glanced.

'Blaencwm's forwards done a tidy job and scrum half Andy Harris come back after a bang on his head which was awful sore.'

I sharpened my red editorial pencil then decided it would be easier to re-write the whole piece in English.

'How did it go love ?' my mother asked me, as if I'd just done my first day in school.

'It's going to be hard work,' I told her.

'Hard work never killed anybody,' she offered.

I nearly asked her if she'd ever heard of the Burma Road, but recalled, just in time, that her father had died there.

As I lay in bed that night, surrounded by bird books, football annuals and Airfix Spitfires, I wondered how I was going to make the Chronicle viable. A hygiene-obsessed ghost and a sports report constructed by placing letters together at random were not exactly what I wanted.

Next morning I called Bob and Sharon together and sat the problem before them.

'We're doing our best,' Bob said.

'I know, but hard work is not enough; we need inspiration.'

'We need a happening,' said Sharon in a Mystic Meg voice. Bob explained to me that Gwladys Benson used to refer to happenings, events beyond the paper's control which, nonetheless, were its lifeline. You can only fill up so many column inches with WI meetings, local court reports and Births, Marriages and Deaths. You need happenings. You need to be in the position of providing big, local news stories to local people.

'Brainstorm ?' Bob said.

'Brainstorm.' Sharon nodded, and they threw themselves to the floor where they lay, on their backs, eyes closed.

I hate brainstorms, almost as much as flipcharts, overhead projectors and psychometric testing.

'Brainstorm.' I repeated, mouthing a silent prayer to the god of all bullshit.

For ten minutes we shouted out ideas and I taped them on my dictaphone. I played it back to my mother that evening.

'Competitions, bingo, old photographs, open access page, schools feature, famous locals, celebrities.'

I shook my head. Mam shook her head. Walter the cat shook his head.

'Why don't you go for a pint ?' my mother asked.

The Rising Sun was an old man's pub, where my father and his father used to meet their mates. When you stepped through the door you stepped back beyond pool tables, juke boxes and quiz machines. Shelves around the walls held the books which made The Sun an unofficial lending library. Everyone sat on wooden chairs around beaten copper tables, catching the warmth of an open fire and reminiscing about times gone by. Whenever anyone struck a match I expected to hear an ARP warden shout, 'Put that ruddy light out.' It was four years since I'd been in there, the day of Dad's funeral, but it hadn't changed. Neville served me with a pint of his warm, gassy bitter and said, 'Are you Willy Jones ?'

'Course I am, Nev,' I said.

'Duw, Duw, ' he enthused. 'There's nice to see you. Home for a spell ?'

Before I could answer he called across the room. 'Handel. Tommy, look who's here, it's Elwyn's boy.'

I went over to where they were sitting and shook their hands.

'Heard you were about..boy,' said Handel.

'Working on the Chronic, I heard,' Tommy said.

'Sorry to hear you're getting divorced.'

'How's your mam's hip ?'

'Essex wasn't it you were living ?'

'Haven't started voting Tory, I hope.'

'Good God mun, Tommy. Hush alive. You'll have his grampa spinning in his grave.'

'No,' I said. 'I'm still as red as you Tommy.'

'Oy,' said Handel. 'Not even Leon Trotsky was as red as old Thomas here.'

They brought me up to date with everything that had happened in Blaencwm in the previous ten years. I thought of asking them to write a column for me; nostalgia sells well with the older ones.

'You've took on a job and a half, haven't you boy ?' Handel asked.

'How's that ?' I said.

'The Chronic,' he said by way of explanation.

'Old Gwlad Benson ran it down with all those bouncing baby photos and bloody jam recipes,' Tommy opined.

'Do you ever read it ?' I enquired, feigning disinterest.

'Never,' they chorused.

It was good to be home and catch up with people I hadn't seen in years. Good too to be able to repay some of my mother's unconditional love. For the first time in my life I found myself talking with my mother about important things: things that mattered, not meaningless trivia. Slowly, but without doubt, we were nursing each other back to health. If only I could do the same for the Chronic.

And then, quite suddenly, it happened: one of Gwladys Benson's happenings, although, I didn't realise at first: I just thought we'd had a bit of snow. Quite a lot, admittedly, but not until Handel claimed it as the worst since 1947 did I recognise it as the happening I had sought. The Rising Sun regulars spent the whole evening recollecting harsh winters: four hours talking about nothing else. The great British obsession, the weather. I walked to work the next morning, the buses being off the roads and wrote up the front page story under the headline:

WORST SINCE '47

I showed Sharon and Bob.

'That's not a happening,' Sharon sneered.

'Listen, I spent four hours in the Rising Sun last night,' I said.

'That would explain it,' Sharon mused, her attitude having matured into playful disrespect.

'All they could talk about was the snow,' I enthused.

'Shall I make with the piccies ?' Bob asked.

'You're there before me Bob,' I smiled.

The week's Chronicle featured 'Arctic Conditions in Heads of Valleys.' One picture, apparently from Siberia showed deserted snow bound streets. Another seemed to be of Polish peasant women queueing for bread outside grim, empty shops. There was the inevitable picture of a slightly bemused sheep rescued by the Territorial Army from under ten foot of the stuff and barely showing gratitude. Well would you ? In January you're an ovine heroine, the poor victim of nature's untamed forces, you capture the hearts of the populace. By April, you're just another roast dinner.

My masterstroke was the headline on page two,

SNOW SPECIAL: 'WORST THIS CENTURY.' SAYS MAYOR

The whole of the district echoed to the sound of a gauntlet being thrown down and I published three letters in the next edition, each nominating the writer's own particular favourite for worst winter of the century.

Mrs. Annie Golding wrote from her log cabin on the tundra above Brynteg to put in a word for February 1933, when she gave birth to her first son in the guard's van of a train stuck in a snow drift on the Old Liner Line assisted by the guard, a boy scout and the midwife from the cottage hospital. It was as she wrote, '...a bitter day and a strange place to bring a child into the world. It was the worst, yet the happiest winter I have ever known.'

Geoffrey Brain wrote from the exile of his beach hut in the South of England where he received his Chronicle by postal subscription.

Sir,

In light of the inclement weather which has beset our district I feel moved to write 'from the boundary.' I recall that much snow fell in February 1933 giving us several days holiday which we whiled away in boyish manner, sledging down tips, skating on the frozen ponds and conducting snowball fights in the quiet streets. However the excellent photographs in last week's edition convinced me that the snow of 1933 was not as severe as this year's. Further, I respectfully suggest that the snow of March 1947 was worse than either. I had returned from the War to live with my father who was postmaster at Blaencwm. Snow covered the shop door and we conducted our business from an upstairs window. Thus, while holding our Mayor in high esteem I am unable to agree that this winter is worse than 1947.

    Yours faithfully
        Geoffrey J. Brain.

The third dispatch came by dog-sled from an igloo near the Volunteers' Park in Blaencwm.

    Dear Sir or Madam,
        I've just about had a feed of hearing the old people going on about how we youngsters don't know the meaning of a cold winter and how we'd never cope if we had to go through what they did and so on and I can just remember the winter of 1962/63 when I was little and it was a very cold winter, much colder than this year and I bet it was colder than 1947 which all those old people keep moaning on about too.

    Love,
    Samantha Lloyd (Miss)

Several of Mam's neighbours came to see me over the weekend, eager to tell me about the winters of 1933, 1947, 1962, 1982, all armed with black and white, mainly white, prints. It dawned on me that I had a winning formula: nostalgia, weather and the sulphurous tang of competition.

Mr. Price-Edwards swept in to the office, puffing heavily

on a ridiculous cigar.

'It's up,' he bellowed.

'I bet your wife's pleased,' Sharon sotto voced from the battered armchair.

'Circulation,' he exclaimed, waving a small piece of paper, Chamberlain fashion. 'Nine point five K.'

'My name's not Kay. It's Sharon.' Sharon said.

'Masterstroke, William boy. Masterstroke. Let's hope we don't get a thaw.'

He breezed out on a trail of cigar smoke and exclamation marks.

'Clever boy Will.,' Sharon mocked. 'So your mam's buying five thousand copies a week now.'

I hardly needed to but in my editorial I invited readers to write about their winter memories. The winner of the star prize was Handel Prosser who had started to buy the Chronicle once more. He claimed that in the bitter winter of 1929 he had stood next to a drunken man who decided to relieve himself on the platform of Blaencwm station only to find that his urine froze into a golden shaft which he proceeded to wave menacingly at a number of young women.

The fourth week we published a special pull-out section: four pages of correspondence on the matter of winter weather. The letter writers were more sophisticated by now, not content merely to nominate their own worst winter, accompanied by some anecdote, methodologies and rationales were being questioned. Alwyn Best M.A. Headmaster of the Comprehensive School wrote, 'There appears to be some inconsistency in selecting criteria by which a winter's relative severity may be assessed. Are we to consider the total snowfall ? The average temperature ? The minimum temperature reached ? Or is some other yardstick to guide our judgement ?'

Which is a fair point after all, and one according to Handel, which someone makes every time the debate takes place and then thinks he is the first person to think of it and therefore a genius.

Mam's hip continued to recover and Aunty Blod said she hadn't seen her looking so well in years. 'It's having you home,' she told me.

Bob, Sharon and I were in the middle of a planning meeting when Mr.Price-Edwards called next, violating the trembling door with the finesse of a visigoth in a Roman brothel and stood there with a smile like a wedge of lemon.

'You have done it,' he exclaimed.

'Only the once, and I didn't enjoy it,' Sharon mugged.

'Done it ?' I asked.

'Last week's edition sold ten point two K.'

'Your mam's parlour must be floor to ceiling with newspapers.' Sharon said to me.

We returned to the office after a small celebratory lunch and Bob had to attend to some negatives in the dark room.

'Our lord and master is rightly pleased with us,' I said. 'We've almost doubled the sales in six weeks and we're having to beat off advertisers with a pointy stick.'

'Can we forget the bloody snow then ?' Sharon asked me. 'I've had it up to here.' She held her hand to her throat.

'That's funny,' I said. 'Because in 1947 there was a snowdrift exactly that deep just outside this very...'

I ducked as she threw a pencil at me. Then we laughed, then smiled at each other. We held each other's gaze for just a little longer than usual.

'Why did you move away from here ?' she asked.

I was going to answer her but couldn't think of a reason. I'd forgotten about my ex-wife. I shifted nervously in my seat and Sharon started to look for her pencil.

Bob timed his entry perfectly. Or maybe not.

'We get our readers to vote on it,' he shouted.

'On what ?' Sharon asked, on her hands and knees.

Being too much of a gentleman to enquire what she was doing on the floor, Bob carried on.

'On the worst winter. We print a sort of ballot paper and they fill it in.'

'We've got to do something,' I agreed. 'It's Easter in a fortnight.'

The headline said it all:
YOU VOTE: '47 WORST... AND IT'S OFFICIAL.'

I opened the first letter addressed to the next Post-bag, and read it to Bob and Sharon.
'Dear Editor, Now that the matter of the worst winter of the century is decided may I suggest that the recent rains have given us the dampest April in living memory. I wonder if other readers have any observations on this matter ?'

'Bob, ' I said, 'get out there with your trusty Nikon and bring me pictures of sodden fields, muddied lambs, rain-beaten daffodils, submerged cricket pitches. I've got a feeling that this one's going to run and run.'

Skedaddling

SALLY HUMBLE-JACKSON

Sally Humble-Jackson began writing five years ago when her three children were very small. She has since published seven novels. She lives in Cardiff.

They don't have hypothermia in Aberdare. It's at a higher altitude than Cardiff and further North, so it's bound to be colder, but the people are warmer which evens it up.

Mind, there's a great deal more central heating in Cardiff. I had a friend who got it when she moved into one of them sheltered flats about ten years ago. It was lovely and warm, but her stuff looked terribly shabby in those modern rooms. She had cream enamel saucepans from before the war and you should have seen them on her fitted-in glass-topped cooker. She said it was like cooking in a time warp. I asked her if it made her mutton taste like lamb and she said knowing her luck it'd be the other way round.

I used to visit her every week. It was awful quiet there. I asked her if they had to wear compulsory slippers when they moved in and she laughed, because she didn't like it anymore than I did. She used to say she envied me still being free and it was true, I was free. I even used to go over there on the bus. I could have afforded a taxi but there was no point. The buses are all right. The drivers don't mind waiting while the geriatrics haul themselves aboard like snails creeping up brick walls; it's all in a day's work to them. It's the passengers who don't like us, though there was always some thin girl with a baby to help me off, so maybe I'm speaking out of turn about that, I don't know. What I do know is, Gwen never went on a bus again after she moved into sheltered. All that central heating and silence sapped her strength.

And, you know, the silly thing was, when she did get ill the warden forced her to go into the hospital anyhow. He said he couldn't take the responsibility, and of course, when you're our age and you go to hospital, you never go home again, no matter what they say.

No, in my opinion I've had ten good years as a result of burying my head in the sand. I wouldn't do it any different even if I'd known I was going to have the fall, and in a way I did know I was going to have the fall because all old ladies fall in the end, don't they ? Usually they break their hips.

I lay on the floor for twenty four hours. Nobody came. Thank goodness. They'd have called an ambulance no matter what I said and I'd've ended up flopped in a chair for the rest of my days, like a blow-up dolly with a puncture watching some old chap fiddling with his catheter pipe and listening to the person in the next chair singing Danny Boy without the words. I was better off on my own.

Mind, it did help that it wasn't my hip, you see, but my wrist. And it was Summer. It all helped.

My hand must've gone numb or something in the end because it stopped hurting for a bit and I managed to get up into my chair. I felt better once I was the right way up again.

I got a good look at it then, of course. It was all puffy and bruised and the hand was crooked; sort of off to one side if you know what I mean. It made me think of the word skedaddle, though I don't know why because I do know what the word skedaddle means. It's just that when I was back up in my chair I kept saying to it, 'You're all skedaddled, you are,' even though I knew the word didn't mean that.

Of course, it started hurting again quite soon after. And it's not much use to me now, that hand, because I never did have the bones set see, but I don't care. If I'd had a plaster they'd have said I couldn't manage to unscrew bottles or something and they'd have carted me off. As it happens, I've managed to do pretty much everything except unscrew bottles, and I never was a great one for pop.

I couldn't go out after that though. That foxed me for a bit. I thought I was going to have to give myself up like a criminal. Dial 999 and tell them to come and take me away. But then I had an idea.

I rung the shop round the corner and asked them to send an order and they did though they don't usually. Barbara Horton brought it herself and said was I all right and I said yes and she started carrying on about fetching the doctor and indeed the next day the doctor shouted through the letterbox and then a social worker turned up and she shouted through the letterbox an'all about how they had care in the community nowadays. I was dead polite to them both, very hoity-toi. I even said the swear words in a posh voice.

When I rung the order through the next week Barbara Horton got upsides with me. She said I was very naughty. She made me want to laugh because even when I was a little girl I'd never been what you'd call naughty.

Mind, I hadn't taken up swearing in them days.

Anyway she gave me a lecture every single week when she brought the food about how I was a worry and shouldn't be so stubborn, but I had the door on the chain and there was nothing she could do. I paid her a delivery charge so we were all square on that account and if she wanted to worry herself sick it wasn't my fault. Anyway, she could see I was all right. I was always compos mentis and there were plenty of things I could eat without unscrewing a bottle.

If you want the truth I was having the time of my life. I ate ham off the greaseproof, chocolate biscuits, listened to the radio, snoozed in front of the electric fire and I re-read all my old books. I even got cheeky enough to ask Barbara Horton to get library books for me after a bit, and she did.

And then one day this punk rock girl brought the order. She said her mother was in hospital. She was a sulky little thing with a ring in her nose. I didn't say anything. If I can get over a broken wrist at my time of life I'm sure she can cope with the odd bout of blood poisoning.

'So what's the matter with your mam ?' I asked. 'Women's troubles ?' And she started to laugh, soft great thing that she is, and she said, 'No, men's troubles, actually. She've got a hernia.'

Anyway, when I get the box inside there's no ham

She came back the next day with the ham. She apologised. She'd forgotten it. I asked after her mam and she dropped her jaw right down and she stuck her tongue in her cheek and she said, actually, well actually, she was in the operating theatre right now this minute. Oh, poor dab. She was frightened to death, she was. Even with all them eyes on I could tell. She couldn't have been more'n fifteen. So I took the chain off and I told her she'd have to make the tea herself and I let her in.

'This kitchen's a tip,' she said.

'Oh, I don't care,' I said. 'I've been cleaning kitchens one way or another for more than eighty years and if God keeps tally he'll judge I've done my bit.'

'Do you believe in God then ?'

Now that was to show how young she was. Give her another couple of years and she wouldn't be caught dead asking a question like that.

'Not really,' I said. 'If I really did believe in him I'd've stopped cleaning kitchens years ago and took up something more godly, wouldn't I ? Mind I do like to picture him up there. It gives me someone to talk to. And if there does turn out to be a day of judgement at least I'll be able to stick up for myself. I can say I had a think about Him now and again. I expect it'll count for something.'

'Do you say prayers then ?'

'I don't get down on my knees, if that's what you mean.'

'Well what do you pray for ?'

'At my time of life ?' I said. 'What do you think ? A man of course.'

She grinned. 'Did he ever send one ?'

'No,' I said. 'He don't answer prayers. Mind, if he did I'd get the shock of my life. I'd have to stop wearing my vest in bed then, wouldn't I ?'

'Why would you have to do that ?'

'Cause it's bad manners to wear your vest under your nightie, didn't you know that ?'

'Oh, it's not bad manners these days. That's old-fashioned that is. You can wear anything in bed these days.'

'Well, remind me to look out for my plastic mac.'

'You're a nutter,' she said. 'Everyone says so.'

'What ? Your mam ?'

'Not just my mum.'

'Oh you mean the social worker. Now let me tell you something my girl. If I live in fear of anyone's day of judgement, it's the social workers. See if they judge you can't cope they put you on a minibus and they send you to hell. They call it the Day Centre.'

She gave me my cup of tea then. 'You're a good laugh you are,' she said.

'This is a terrible cup of tea.'

She put on her sulky face then. 'I tried my best.'

'Did you ? Good job you're not my age then. If this was the best you could manage at my age you'd end up in an old people's home with an incontinence pad on.'

Anyway, she always brought the order after that. I didn't let her in every week because I didn't always feel like talking to her. She was a silly girl. I bet she got on her mother's nerves.

But you couldn't help liking her though.

Then one week she come and she'd taken the ring out of her nose. She'd been crying her eyes out and it must've been rubbing when she blew her nose because it was all pink and swollen round the hole.

'You'd better come in,' I said.

She came in but then she went all quiet on me when I asked what the matter was.

'Boyfriend trouble ?' I suggested. 'You should do yourself up a bit you know. I know they say they don't care what you look like but they do really. They're all mouth men.'

She looked daggers at me when I said that. He face was all grey blotches from the eye make-up.

'Actually,' she said, very haughty. 'Actually, if you must know, I'm leaving school.'

'Are you ?'

'I'm getting a flat.'

'Oh aye ?'

'With a friend.'

'Well there's nice.'

'A male friend.'

I laughed out loud. I couldn't help myself. I was so surprised.

'You mean you've got a fellow who wants to wake up next to you every morning with you looking like that ? With all them eyes on and that ring through your nose.'

'What's there to laugh at ?'

'Oh nothing, I don't suppose. At least you know what it is he's interested in so you won't be disappointed. In my day we wanted romance. We wanted to be swept off our feet.'

'Girls today aren't like that.' She'd gone red. Red and grey. 'We've got as much right to sexual pleasure as anyone.'

'Anyone ?' I said 'Does that include me ?'

'You know what I mean,' she muttered, but I didn't really. I'm from the wrong generation for sex.

'So what does your mam say about it all?'

She pulled one of her faces. 'I can do what I like. I'm old enough.'

'You want to watch you don't end up with a baby. You're old enough for that an'all.'

'I'm on the pill.'

'Well let's hope you're old enough to remember to take it, eh?'

I don't think she knew how to take me really. I think she was expecting me to tell her not to ruin her life.

I just filled the kettle.

She watched me do it.

'What's the matter with your hand?'

'Oh I've always had this hand,' I said. 'I was born with it.'

'My mum said you had a fall.'

'And your mam knows everything, do she? She's always right I suppose?'

She was just about to agree with me when she caught my eye. At least she had the grace to laugh.

So I had to go back to having Barbara Horton bring the order for a bit and give me the lectures. I didn't let her in. And to tell the truth I was on tenterhooks about that girl, I really was, because you don't like to see them make a mess of their lives. Do you? Even when you know they've got their heart set on it.

And then after a couple of months she turns up again, very sheepish.

'I'm living back at home,' she mumbled.

Do you know, she'd got a chain looped from her ear-ring right across her face to the ring on her nose.

'Do you know what you look like?' I said. 'You look like

a brooch. With a safety chain.'

'I might get the other nostril done next week.'

'Oh, that'll be lovely, that will. Keep your nose chained up then there's no danger of it falling off.'

Silence.

'Or are you wearing it to frighten the fellows away ? Like me with the chain on my door ?'

'I might be.'

'Oh, you don't want to let one bad egg put you off. You'll soon get another boyfriend. You've got a kind heart, you have. That's what counts.'

I embarrassed her saying that. She started to pick the black varnish off her nails.

'You're a nutter you are,' she said.

'Am I ?'

'Everyone else thinks I'm terrible. Don't you disapprove of what I did ?'

'Any reason why I should ?'

'I dunno. God ? You half-believe in Him after all.'

'Oh, I believe in Him completely these days,' I told her. 'But I wouldn't worry about what He thinks if I was you. You can stick up for yourself with anyone if you've a mind to. He likes people who do that. He likes anyone who's got a bit of nerve.'

Oh, you should have seen her face when I said that. It was the right thing to say, it really was. She put the kettle on. And at least she'd learned to make a decent cup of tea in that flat.

She never asked me why I'd changed my mind about God, which is a good job really because I wouldn't have told her. I'm not telling anyone about the pains in my chest but they do get worse every time which is good. With any luck I'll be in my chair with my library book tucked up my jumper and a chocolate biscuit in my hand. When I don't phone my order through her mam'll guess; she'll send the social worker round to shout through the letterbox again. But I won't care will I ? I'll have skedaddled by then.

The Wild Service Tree

SIMON REES

Simon Rees' published work includes *The Devil's Looking-Glass* (1985), *Making a Snowman* (1990) and *Nathaniel and Mrs.Palmer* (1991) published by Methuen and Penguin. His stories and poems have appeared in a range of publications. He wrote the script for *Soul of a Nation* and has made singing translations of three operas. He lives in Cardiff and works for the Welsh National Opera.

Polly Nightingale walked briskly, like a thief on an errand, along the footpath leading to the bridge over the canal. The fast-flowing, muddy water in its channel was fringed with something-gigantea: vast, rhubarb-like leaves the size of umbrellas with prickly stems. She knew it was properly called the Dock Feeder, and that having gurgled through its sluice at Blackweir below the little suspension bridge that bounced as you crossed it, outlined the length of Bute Park and acted momentarily as a moat to the castle. It would gurgle once more through a second sluice, flow under the city and only emerge by the railway tracks to pour unromantically into the East Bute Dock. Knowing this, however, did not stop Polly from finding the canal attractive; she loved the dark water and its purposeful motion, uneddied and unwhirlpooled, that led as smoothly as a tarmac road towards its destination, even its destiny, topping up the dock. Whenever she came up up to the Park from Atlantic Wharf, she felt the presence of the water under her feet, like a gravity-wave tugging at her flat-heeled shoes, and sending powerful currents up her calves and out at her shoulders, keeping them firmly back, squared under her tarpaulin jacket with its neat brown corduroy collar.

Today she carried a bag, in grubby off-white cotton with a print of the Bodleian Library, a present from her sister, who worked there. An empty shopping-bag, taken towards the market and the stores, indicates a green and disciplined spirit, one that embodies forethought and a conservationist care.

Empty, it fluttered and unfurled against her skirt, and made her feel less guilty about her raiding mission, one she felt must be clearly visible to any passer-by.

Spurred by a recipe in a thumbed Jane Grigson cookbook, she had decided to remove from the arboretum as many pounds of crab apples, rowan berries, hips, haws, sloes, medlars, quinces and other assorted fruit as she could make off with uncaught. Stolen fruit is sweetest. These harsh drupes and berries she would pick over, clean, sweeten and steep in spirit, the cheapest, strongest vodka or brandy, to produce a series of liqueurs or ratafias that would give the winter months something to look forward to. A pungent, tonic cordial that would quicken the blood and warm the cockles of the heart. It was no use looking for such fruit in the market, as nobody sold them. As for her garden, the handkerchief-sized patch of clay and rubble would yield nothing but stunted buddleias and spiny berberis, not even the fruiting kind whose sour purple ink-pellets the Persians used to flavour their rice and lamb pilaus. "I want a pilau without any feathers," she'd overhead from a loutish lad in the Indian take-away the other day; odd how such phrases stick in the mind. Anyway, what better to take away the aftertaste of a take-away than something sweet and strong ? Out of the strong came forth sweetness, like the lion on the label of the golden-syrup can.

She had strode through the shoppers, wondering what they would think of her planned activity, no better than shoplifting, to be perfectly honest, and whether the sight of her carrying the half-dozen bottles of liquor she'd need would make any of them smirk or frown. Spinsters and the brandy-bottle: the joke went back to Queen Anne, probably to Good Queen Bess. Unhappy old maids, tippling through the night, to fall into a drunken stupor just before the dawn, and sleep till noon. Not her: early to bed, early to rise, that was her motto.

The park was practically empty, thank god. She took a

branching path along the Dock Feeder, hollow cement egg-boxes set into the turf to let the grass grow through, and tried to keep her heels from catching in the cavities; it was like walking on rotten molars. Her own back doubles were playing up, the fillings conducting heat and cold far more than she was used to; and, for a paradox, she was cutting her wisdoms as well, which threatened to impact. More pain, more expense, just what she could do without after... but what was the point on dwelling on that ?

The trees in the arboretum looked promising; the cherries had lost their leaves and stood stark and oriental. The maples and sycamores were colouring up, but who gave a damn? All they bore were withered, rattling twisted keys that fell in pathetic spirals, not even flying far from the trunk. Then there were the fruiting trees, covered to one degree or another with stippled dots of fruit, yellow and orange and red, with the startling clusters of rowan berries brightest of all. She could imagine their taste in her mouth, and the saliva ran.

She had filled her bag nearly to the brim with golden crab apples the size of cherries; medlars, with skins like scuffed book-bindings; three quinces, whose fragrance rose from the jet-black mottling that gave them an ormolu look, and a couple of bunches of rowans to top the lot, nodding on their stems and looking as gaudy as enamel. Then she saw another group of trees, ones she had not harvested or even visited before, standing in a clump inside an elbow of the path. She went up to the first of them, drawn by its chequered bark and purplish-red foliage, reached her hand into the branches and drew down a cluster of berries. The fruit was a light tan, speckled like pigskin, and oblong in shape. She bit one and let the acid pulp spread across her tongue. The seeds were hard and smooth, and she spat them into her palm. The rest of the fruit had a gritty, sandy quality, and dried her tongue and the insides of her cheeks until she felt her mouth must pucker with the sudden astringency.

'They call them chequerberries,' said a voice behind the tree. Polly dropped her shopping bag, and the fruit spilled out like a harvest festival display.

'That's a good haul you've got there. Let me help you pick them up, since I made you drop them.'

'No, I...' Polly squatted down on her heels to gather the fruit, not waiting to look up and discover a policeman, a tramp, a park-keeper, a pervert, a jogger, a mugger, a plain-clothes detective or a child molester. Her face felt as red as the reddest of the fruit. The man stood there, moleskin trousered over brogues, good brogues too, their perforated toecaps polished with oxblood and unstained by the damp grass. She looked up further to see a fawn-coloured duffel-coat, a deerstalker cap and a pair of horn-rimmed glasses over a grizzled beard. The face was dust-shot with tiny dark flecks, and looked like the fruit she had taken from the tree, acid and dry to bite into.

'Do you know the name of the tree ?'

Polly used both hands to pick up the last of the fruit, and levered herself into a standing position.

'No, I don't, and if you don't mind...'

'Sorbus torminalis, the wild service tree. Otherwise known as hagberry, hezzony, whitty-bush or chequers, depending on where you're from.'

'Very interesting. Do you normally lurk behind trees and surprise people with your erudition ?'

'I read it up in Geoffrey Grigson.'

'How funny. I'm getting stuff together for a recipe by his wife, or his widow.'

'They hunted in couples, I believe. Swapped notes, that sort of thing.'

His left hand bore no wedding ring, but he seemed well-kempt and unbachelorish, except for the deerstalker. Wearing a cap and a hooded coat together seemed eccentric, but not actually mad.

'Are you a specialist in trees ?'

'Not exactly.'

'You aren't the gardener? Or whatever they call it, there must be a grander name. The arboriculturalist or something ?'

'No, I don't work here. I don't work anywhere. I've moved here in my retirement. My wife and I sold up in Sevenoaks and bought a flat in Richmond Road.'

'And then she died ?'

'And then she died.'

'Long ago ?'

'Long enough.'

Long enough to be out on the prowl for women of a similar age and set of interests ? Why not ? Why not ? They walked together along the path, back towards the castle..

'My name's Astley. Gerard Astley. I'm sure you can work out my nickname.'

'I'm Polly Nightingale.'

'Now if my surname had been Rose...'

'I'm always meeting Roses. I've known quite a few. Names draw people to each other, and then when you've looked for a while, you realise there's nothing there except the sound and the association.'

'A Rose by any other name?'

'Exactly.' It was like the matching of a bacterium to antibody, key to lock, this setting up of codes to be decoded, passwords to check and countercheck. Capping references established which zone of the language map this other one inhabited, where he roamed and felt free, where he was restricted and fenced in. Here one found botany, literature, nomenclature, along with moderate prosperity, a non-smoker's breath, though there must have been a pipe at some period, to have yellowed and snaggled the teeth, and drawn down to the corner of the mouth and a lively gait, no arthritic catchings or lurchings, no heart watching hesitancy or dragging of the step.

'Besides onomastics and taxonomy.' She looked at him to check for eyes glazing over, a puckering of the chin.

'What are my other interests ? Oh, I've been a book-dealer, antiquarian of course; what other kind is there ? And I've travelled back and forth a lot to the States. That's all over now, though, speaking professionally.'

'Speaking professionally, I wouldn't have said it ever could be.'

'You're a psychiatrist ?'

'A counsellor.'

'Physician, heal thyself, eh ?'

'What makes you say that ?'

'You want some more human contact, outside the forum of work.'

'You think I come out to the park to pick up strangers?'

'There's a difference between gathering windfalls and pulling fruit straight off the branches.'

'Tell me about the wild service tree.'

They had come to the bridge over the Dock Feeder, beside where the paths divided. A natural break, an easy, unforced, though wished for, parting of the ways could be engineered at this point with the minimum expense of will power. The water flowed oilily, thickly, with red and yellow maple leaves rotating as they glided, like an exercise in topological transformations.

'What a fabric pattern that would make.'

'What a print for an end-paper.'

'You could bind a book in that colour, with the leaves appliqued into grey calfskin.'

'Or stamped in gold and silver foil.'

'Oh, no, far too gaudy.'

'Thanks.'

'On second thoughts, it could look quite grand and splendid. Something for a volume of epitaphs, or Japanese haiku.'

'I can see you know what I mean.'

'Tell me about the wild service tree.'

Astley folded his hands on the rail. They were gloved in brown calf with a tawny coloured amber button at the wrist, and without the three branched stitching on the back that always reminded Polly of a childish, schematic attempt to draw the Prince of Wales' feathers.

'It's one of the rarest British trees. This specimen will have been brought in from the wild, but you can buy them from nurseries. The bark peels off in squarish flakes and strips, leaving a pale under-bark, and hence the name of chequers. Only the confusion comes from the fruit, which are also chequered and speckled, like guineafowl or snakes-head fritillaries.'

"I love you," thought Polly. "Don't stop. Go on."

'So it might be named from the bark or the fruit, you see.'

'Where does the 'service' come from?'

'It's a corruption of sorbus. It's grown here since Roman times. The Welsh name is pren criafol. They used to burn it for charcoal. That's why it's nearly died out.'

'Where can you get them?'

'As I said, nurseries, plantsmen, garden suppliers. Do you want one?'

'I don't know. I'd have to grub out some of the berberis.'

'Extirpate it, root and branch. I'll come and dig it out for you. I'll bring a fork and a shovel and my gardening gloves.'

Polly touched the back of his hand.

'Tougher than these?'

'Much tougher. I'll bring a wheelbarrow.'

'In your car?'

'No, I'll trundle it across town.'

'From Richmond Road to Atlantic Wharf?'

'Why not? Is that where you live? I've tracked you down. You'll be in the phone-book. How many Nightingales in Butetown? Not so many. I can ring around.'

'I'll tell you where I live,' said Polly, 'but don't come round at once. I want to walk past your flat a couple of times first.'

'Throw a service-berry into the front garden. See if it grows.'

'That would take too long, wouldn't you say?'

'I don't know. They're quick to germinate. How long will your liquor take to mature?'

'I don't know. What is it now? October? Wait until after Christmas, early New Year.'

'That's long enough. You give me a bottle of spirit, I'll plant you a sapling. How does that sound?'

'It sounds fine.'

'We're both newcomers, but we can take our time.'

Polly took an involuntary look at her watch. So late.

'I'd better go. You know where I am.'

'I can find out. Do you want my phone number?'

'No I'll leave it....leave it to you.'

'Give me one of those berries you've got in your bag.'

She took out a service-berry, the chequer-berry, and gave it to him. He bit it in too, revealing the pale pulp and paired black seeds, pocketed one half and gave her the other. She fumbled to hold it, letting her fingertips explore the dry skin and the moist interior, the bristled husk at the calyx, the wiry stalk. Astley bowed to her, stiffly, from the waist.

'Goodbye, then.'

'Goodbye.'

They walked away from each other, down the separate paths.

The Call of Duty

HERBERT WILLIAMS

Herbert Williams is a freelance writer of poetry, fiction and biography while also creating plays for television and radio. His recent short story collection *The Stars in their Courses* is published by Alun Books.

B lake stood on the promenade, watching the tide come in.
He was in no hurry to move; the job was done, more or
less to his satisfaction, and the prospect of a return home
was not inviting.

The sea, for him, was an unfamiliar sight. He encountered
it, typically, in lunging immersions on holiday islands; it was an
invigorating experience, not a subject for reflection. Now,
however, he found himself looking at it in a new way. He was
intrigued by its slow, deliberate progress. It touched a chord in
him, since he too had this steady deliberation. Above all it was
irresistible, but this was a quality he could not match.

Blake was a large, florid man with a hairstyle borrowed
from the footballers of his youth: parted in the middle, it lay flat
against his skull, so that it seemed not so much a growing thing
as a cosmetic addition. His body was still muscular, his hands
broad and practical.

There were few people on the prom. The holiday season
was over, and the small resort once again inert and private; the
intrusion of visitors had not ruffled its inner security, the
anachronistic calm which made it a haven for the retired and a
constant reproach to modernity. If Blake had been of a constant
reproach to modernity. If Blake had been of a philosophical cast
of mind, he might have reflected on the irony of the contrast
between his mission and these surroundings, but it was only
because he was otherwise that the mission had been his at all.

Now it was accomplished, he felt the usual sense of relief.

It might have been done better, of course, but few men are perfect. He aimed for efficiency of execution and was judged by the results. Rarely did he disappoint, in a field where there was only a small margin for human error. In the old days, he would not have lingered so long in the area, but Blake had learned the value of disguise by normality, the ability not to be noticed simply because he did nothing to avoid attention.

It was the stillness of the girl that first caught his eye. There was movement all around her. Gulls swirling, the sea fretfully lapping the gritty sand. But she sat perfectly motionless on the rocks, her back turned to the prom in a squat, dismissive way. Something about her attitude disturbed him and something about her, too. For although he could not see her face he was reminded, he knew not why, of his daughter Claire.

Unconsciously, his grip on the promenade railing tightened. She had been dead ten years, a life snuffed out by an overdose of drugs doled out too readily by an overworked practitioner. He still resented it: the professional hand scribbling lines on a small piece of paper; lines intelligible only to another professional, busy among white-coated assistants in a clinical den, all perfectly respectable. Two highly regarded professionals, unintentionally conspiring to provide a confused, unhappy young woman of nineteen with the means to destroy herself.

He was about to move on, throwing off the past as best he could, when the girl stood up. She did so abruptly, as if a decision had been made, and began walking over the rocks towards the sea. They were low rocks, easily crossed; to step from one to another required no great effort. Blake noticed, so keenly was his gaze fixed upon her, that she seemed hardly to look down at all. Head up, she made her way towards the sea, and Blake now was as motionless as she had been a moment before.

It was only when she actually stood in the water that his

mouth dried. He swayed a little, and a pulse in his temple began to beat. She was still again, momentarily, and then she resumed her walk. He tried to call out but no sound came; he was as one cast in stone. Then, with a shuddering impulse, he vaulted over the railings and ran down the beach, shouting.

She seemed not to hear him and, even to himself, his voice was detached and impersonal, uttering sounds of which he hardly knew the meaning. He was a being catapulted into action by a fierce necessity, no longer Blake but a channel through which the life force tried to connect with the girl in the sea. The water now, was above her knees, touching the hem of her short skirt. He feared that, any moment, she might be sucked under. 'Stop,' he cried. 'Stop.' But still she walked on.

At the water's edge, he was suddenly filled with a sense of authority. Who was she, this unknown girl, to defy him, Blake, a commander of destiny? Filling his lungs, he boomed: 'You. Out there. Stop, do you hear me?' And for the first time, he knew that his voice registered. She paused, the sea flowing past her thighs. She half turned, struggling to stay upright, and Blake saw this as a small triumph, an assertion of power. For the first time he saw her profile, the pale vulnerability of her features, and called out, 'Wait there. Don't move.' Like figures in a tableau they stood, transfixed. And then she turned, rejecting him.

It happened quickly, yet afterwards he was amazed that so much detail stayed with him. She stumbled, falling forward into the sea. He splashed through the shallows, lifting her out bodily and carrying her back to the shore. He bent her over, thumping her back, and then she coughed and heaved and retched, spewing seawater out on to the dry sand. At last she stood up, shivering, and he took off his jacket and wrapped it around her shoulders before encircling her in his arms, comforting her.

They remained so for what seemed a long time. A voice

began speaking inside him, telling him to go. But he held her firmly, triumphantly, a man in touch again with his past.

At last she drew away. Her eyes were blue-grey. Steady eyes. Not at all like Claire's.

'Who the hell are you ?' she said.

'Does it matter ?'

'It does to me.'

'My name's Blake,' he said.

'Well Blake,'she said, her voice cracking, 'why the hell don't you mind your own business ?'

And then she wept.

They trudged up the beach side by side, saying nothing. No-one on the prom appeared to have seen anything untoward. It gave Blake the weird feeling that neither him or the girl existed. If he hadn't been there, she'd have drowned. And he was there only because of the job. That was the strangest thing of all.

A short flight of wooden steps led up to the prom. Blake waved the girl forward; she smiled faintly and went first.

'Proper gentleman, aren't you ?' she said at the top.

He looked at her questioningly.

'Letting me go first. One of the old school, that it?'

'Something like.'

She wriggled her jacket off her shoulders, handed it back.

'Thank you,' she said. 'For nothing.' And began walking away.

'Where are you going now?'

'Home. Where'd you think?'

'You're soaking wet. I'll give you a lift.'

'Get stuffed.'

'What?'

She turned, her face contorted. 'Look. Because you saved my bloody life, Mr Nosey-Parker Blake, it doesn't mean you can screw me, OK?'

He stared at her, astonished.

'So just...' She swayed, deathly pale, and stepping quickly forward he steadied her.

'Oh shit,' she said hopelessly. 'Aren't I just bloody pathetic?'

Sitting next to him in the front passenger seat, she shivered convulsively. His wet clothes, clinging to him, squeezed the sea into his bones but inside himself he felt warm and strange, as if he had come alive again.

He had put his jacket back around her shoulders.

'Oh god,' she kept murmuring. 'Oh god. Oh god.'

'Don't worry,' he said. 'Just don't worry. Shall I take you to hospital?'

Her eyes opened wide. 'Hospital? What for?'

'Well, you're in need of treatment.Obviously.'

'Like hell I am.'

He started the engine. 'Which way ?'

'Bangor Terrace.'

'I don't know where that is.'

'Christ. Just move, that's all. Move.'

At a mini-roundabout, he turned right. A policeman, standing on the corner, stared at them. Blake gave him a nod. The policeman ignored him.

He ought to be getting along now. Out of North Wales. Back to base. According to instructions. He'd take her home, then leave.

She was shuddering now, not simply with the cold.

'Where now?'

'What?'

'Which turning next?'

She looked up, only half-seeing. 'Right. No, left. Next left. No... next but one. Then right.'

She closed her eyes again. Somehow they got there.

'Well,' he said. 'Here we are.'

It had been a steep climb, up a twisting road to a row of three-storey houses half-way up the hill behind the resort. There were small, scrubby front gardens behind cast-iron railings which, like the houses themselves, were badly in need of a coat of paint. They were once smart homes of the bourgeoisie, socially diminished and parceled out as flats and bedsits.

By now she had stopped shivering.

'Hey,' he said. 'Wake up. We're home.'

Her eyes flicked open and she looked at him, strangely calm.

'Come along then,' she said. 'I'll find you some dry clothes.'

Taken by surprise, he returned her gaze. She was thirtyish, he supposed, the sort of age Claire would have been now, but other than that there was little physical resemblance. She was the fragile fair English rose; Claire had been the dark Welsh-Iberian.

He shook his head. 'Can't, I'm afraid. I've got to be going. I just wanted to make sure...'

'Don't be silly,'she cut in. 'You can't drive on like that. You'll catch your death.'

As if on cue, he shivered.

'Come on,' she said. 'You can have a bath.'

They climbed two flights of stairs. As she turned the yale key to her flat, it struck him that this was the first time he would have been in a strange woman's place since Dora. His wife had been alive by then. Dora had been about the same age as themselves, one of the fleeting adventures which, for a certain period of his life, had given him amusement.

At a glance he took in the books, the paintings, the colour supplement furnishings.

He looked out of the tall window, which reached almost from ceiling to floor. Over the sea, a pale yellow light filtered through high, herringbone clouds. The Costa Geriatrica, he thought grimly. Just the place for me, one day.

He turned. She was staring at him, as if seeing him for the first time.

'Why did you do it?' she said.

'I might ask you the same thing.'

'You had no right. I wanted to die.'

'Why?'

'That's my business.'

He shrugged.

'I'm taking a shower,' she said. 'You can go in after.'

Soaking himself in the bath, he seemed to breathe the essence of her. Now, she no longer reminded him of Claire; she had achieved an identity of her own. He seemed to see her under the shower, her pale skin covered with tiny globules of water that ran slowly down her body. She tilted her head back; her angular breasts jutted out, their nipples sharply profiled. He sponged himself vigorously, to obliterate the image. It returned, insistently; he got out of the bath and roughly dried himself with the too soft towel.

She had changed into smart jeans, a light blue shirt. There was a cafetiere on the table, two mugs, a bowl of brown sugar.

She looked him up and down, smiled wryly. 'Not too bad a fit, considering.'

'Bespoke, I'd say.'

'Not quite.'

The trousers dug into his waist, the shirt might have

served as an apprentice straitjacket.

'At least they're dry,' he conceded. 'Whose are they? Or shouldn't they ask?'

'Dad's.' Again, fleetingly she was Claire, and then herself again. 'He stays here sometimes. Leaves a few things hanging about.'

Blake grunted.

'White or black?'

'White.'

'I'll leave you put sugar in. If you want it.'

He had another hour there at the most. Then he would have to leave. Absolutely.

He stirred in the sugar. She looked at him thoughtfully, both hands clasping the mug.

'I suppose I ought to say thank you.'

'You needn't. If you don't want to.'

'I've never done it before.'

'I should hope not.'

'But I've thought about it a lot.'

Again he grunted.

'What do you do?' she asked. 'I mean, who are you?'

'I told you.'

'Blake. Mr.Blake. That doesn't say much.'

He sipped his coffee, giving nothing away.

'Are you on holiday, or what?'

'That's it,' he smiled, smiling bleakly. 'I'm on holiday.'

'No you're not,' she said slowly. 'If you were...' She left the sentence unfinished. 'So what do you do? Tell me.'

'I mind my own business.'

'Ouch.'

The flip word annoyed him. What was he doing, lingering here with this crazy woman, wearing her father's clothes, drinking her coffee? He had to be on his way. Losing himself.

He began gulping the coffee, stinging his tongue.

'What's wrong ?' she said. 'I've upset you, have I?'

'Not in the least.'

'Yes I have. What is it, something I've said?'

He shook his head.

'I'm sorry. Whatever it is, I'm sorry. Believe me.'

Her eyes were moist. Her voice held the suspicion of a tremor.

'Don't worry,' he said. 'You haven't done anything.'

'No. Not much.'

She put down the mug, dabbed her eyes.

'Look,' he said. 'I have to be going. I'm very sorry, but I'm here on business. I've got things to do.'

'That's all right. I understand. Only it's just...'

He wanted to say: What? But did not.

She blew her nose.

Again memories of Claire surged back. Her saying, 'I'm all right, Daddy. Really. I'm quite all right.'

When she had not been. Patently.

Blake said, 'Why did you do it? Why try to top yourself?'

Her eyes, after the tears, had a steely glitter.

'The usual,' she said at last. 'It's so banal.'

'A boy?'

'Man,' she corrected. 'I'm thirty-four.'

He almost said, 'I didn't think you were that much,' but stopped himself.

'Married,' said Blake gently. 'Was he ?'

She nodded. 'I told you. It's entirely banal.'

'Are you?' she added.

'I was. My wife died six years ago.'

She did not say: I'm sorry.

They lapsed into silence. Blake looked around, fixing the room in his mind. Fixing her.

131

She seemed, now, almost unaware of him. She was looking into something he could not penetrate.

'Look,' he said gently. 'I've really got to be going. If you could give me my clothes back...'

'They won't be dry yet,' she said. 'But they'll be better than they were, that's for sure.'

She brought them to him. He clutched their damp warmth, took them into the bathroom.

When he came out, the radio was on. He wondered if she'd be listening to it later in the evening.

She gave him a strange look. 'Where are you going now?'

'Home,' he said, echoing the answer she had given him earlier.

'Where's home ?'

'South Wales,' he lied.

'That's a big place. Can't you be more specific?'

'Cardiff.'

'Cardiff,' she repeated. 'Mr.Blake of Cardiff. Nice.'

'Are you all right now?' he asked.

'Yes. I'm fine.'

'Sure now?'

She nodded.

'Not going to try that nonsense again, are you? He's never worth it, you know. Whoever he is.'

'Don't worry.'

He frowned. 'Your parents should know about this. Are you going to tell them?'

'There's only dad.'

'Well. Him then. You going to tell him?'

'Of course not.'

'Why not ?'

'He's got enough on his plate. He's a busy man. Like you.'

'Why?' he said, without thinking. 'What's he do ?'

'Oh,' she replied smiling faintly. 'This and that.'

He felt an almost overpowering urge to kiss her.

'Well,' he said gruffly, 'thanks for drying my things. It was very kind of you.'

'Not at all. It's the least I could do.'

They stood in silence a moment, aware of the absurdity of their courtesies.

'Goodbye then.' He extended his hand.

She did not shake it but held it, between both of hers.

'Goodbye,'she said. 'Mr.Mystery Man.'

'Why do you call me that?'

'Because you are. Aren't you ?'

She looked at him teasingly.

At the very last moment, he saw the letter on the hallstand.

'Who's that for?' he asked wonderingly.

'My father, of course,' she said. 'Who else?'

When the newsflash came on the car radio, hours later, he had that sense of unreality, that so huge, so expected a thing should actually happen. Then he laughed, an eruption of pure physical joy. Once again he had done it; life and death lay in his gift. The bomb had done its work; the bastard was dead, blown to bits in his yacht on the Costa Geriatrica.

He had not forgotten her, how could he? But he felt no sense of guilt, nor even pity. To save one, destroy the other. A hand, greater even than his, decided all such matters.

Mrs Kuroda on Penyfan

NIGEL JARRET

Nigel Jarret was born in Gwent. His prose and poetry have appeared in several of Britain's major literary magazines and he is the co-editor of a book about the Victorian writer, Arthur Machen. He has been a journalist for twenty seven years, currently at the South Wales Argus. He lives at Llanvaches, near Newport.

S olemn over fertile country floats the white cloud.

Mrs Kuroda remembered these words from the diary she had kept as a teenager, and now they seemed to be written in the skies, signalling to her personally a truth so long untold. In those days, she kept lots of similar things; newspapers cuttings, snippets from books, tattered pictures of the Western World. Each will come true, she had told herself, each will materialise.

Smithereens. She had learnt that word from Bill while they were underground at the mining museum. Ichiro, her husband, hadn't been bothered at all. 'Look after her Bill,' he had said, emphasising the man's name as though he had been practising it all night for some important leave taking ceremony at which his face would be creased, all smiling. That was why he had done so well for himself, Mrs.Kuroda thought. His determination to succeed in that windswept, hilly land among its emotional people would see them through. Forty years before, in Nagasaki, these were the qualities which mothers-to-be seemed to will on their unborn children in the anguish of bringing them into the world. Mothers who had survived, of course. 'Blown to smithereens,' Bill had said while recounting the tale of the pit disaster. It was almost as if Ichiro had instructed him to mention it, in order to impress on his wife the triumph of similarity over difference.

Alone in their house in the Vale, she stared at her face in the dressing-table mirror, vaguely aware of the double reflection looking in from its two side panels. In front of her was the photograph. The whole effect was that of a shrine, in which she and her mirror images were fixed, not the gazer but the gazed upon. Ichiro had taken the photo with one of his firm's remote-control cameras just before they came to Wales. 'Sachi, my dearest' he had written on it. That was what he called her in private. Now, in their new country, he used it in public instead of Sachiko, which seemed to her like something cast off by another against her will, or something surrendered reluctantly at Customs.

She collected her walking-boots, so tiny they made her smile, and placed them on the back seat of her car with the bobble hat and the windcheater. The company had provided them with a big house on its own in the country. It was too big really, but there was a lot of entertaining involved in being Mrs.Kuroda. Ichiro had taken ages to choose. At each likely property, in similar locations to the one he had finally picked, he would race to the first upstairs window, then to the highest point in the garden if it weren't flat, and train his binoculars on the horizon. Only at their chosen site did he obtain a view of a green landscape unfolding tumultuously into purple-saddled hills and jagged spoil heaps. One wintry morning, not long after their arrival, Ichiro woke her and led her excitedly to the bedroom window, offering her the glasses. The tip above distant pontmoel was snow-capped. 'Mount Fuji,' he cried.

Mrs Kuroda's Mazda showed the beginning of rust at its hem. She drove it through the gates and let it roll down the slope, through the tunnel of trees. It had been another of Ichiro's ideas for her to buy a second-hand car which would demonstrate that she was neither ostentatious nor concerned to present all things Japanese as faultless. 'In any case,' he had told her, 'this is the car of our people.' Our people meaning the workers at his Pontmoel electronics factory. She went along with these harmless subterfuges. Ichiro's energy made her breathless. He was so sure of himself that she was swept along by his enthusiasm. She had the feeling of being always in his wake, but an affectionate smile over his shoulder every so often would re-assure her. He knew all this; he was conscious of having to look back every time he craved her sweet, doll-like features. That was how the sinecure had come about. That was why he had placed her in charge of the Home Club, for the company's middle-management.

There were tears welling when she pulled up at the city junction, ready to drive north to the Brecon Beacons, and they broke like dammed waters as she giggled at the small roadside hoarding. BILL POSTERS WILL BE PROSECUTED, it said in bold multiples. Bill had explained the joke, which hadn't been all that difficult to understand with her good command of English, but she had not found it as funny as he had. It wasn't all so unproductive where she and Bill were concerned. He had begun by telling her about Welsh past and the need to embrace a different Welsh future. He'd told her that her face was like the dawn, on the afternoon he'd introduced her to the story of the ill-fated Gelert. She laughed again through her tears as she recalled her comical attempts at pronunciation. 'Smith-er-eens, Mab-in-og-ion,' she had repeated between her little high pitched cries of glee. Ichiro had heard her practicing the words in the kitchen.

'What's that, Sachi?' he had called from the doorway, lowering his opened newspaper to waist height.

'Oh, nothing,' she had replied. 'More English sayings.'

Mrs Kuroda had worked hard at her job. Turning up the valley parallel to the one where Ichiro was at the moment addressing the assembled workforce on the impending need for redundancies, she heard the Home Club documents on the back seat cascade on to the floor like a column of slates. She didn't care. Her tears were as much for poor Dr Kagoshima, due to arrive from the Osaka plant at the weekend, as they were for anyone else, including herself. Even Dr Kagoshima, coming with bad news from the East but due to be confronted with all that was positive in his Western empire, even the modest Pontmoel Home Club, could not take her far enough back. She remembered a scene from a film in which a teenage boy waited in vain for the return of the suicide pilots then clambered into the cockpit himself, white headband trailing, only for the engine to fail. It might have been old Dr Kagoshima. Both of them in their own ways had been born too late for the big events.

She pulled in at a lay-by which led down to the side of a small reservoir. It was where she and Bill had gone after the visit to the museum. 'My recent past', he had called it. How thrilled she had been at the success of those first meetings. Ideas and suggestions drifted against the Club's slender administrative structure, almost suffocating it with potential. In the dark evenings she would sit at home under the standard lamp with her glasses balanced on the tip of her nose and map out the Club's course, while her husband, stretched out on the settee, examined the Financial Times in microscopic detail. She felt there was a sense in which he had found her something with which to occupy herself and was loath to intrude unduly.

One night, after a committee change caused by illness, she wrote the name William Posters in a vacant space in her minutes book. 'Do you know him, Ichiro ?' she asked, without looking up.

'No, oh, yes,' he replied, and turned the page of his paper.

There were three ducks on the choppy waters, bobbing together against a stiff wind. A thousand wavelets broke together. Hers was the only car in the gravelled parking bay. She put on her bobble hat and walked towards the water's edge, wrapping her arms around her to keep warm. For every wave a thought, collapsing to make room for another. The endless succession wearied her; the wind almost carried her away. She remembered giving Bill that first lift home after they had stayed late to discuss the home club's Summer programme. It was he who had suggested the Japanese evening, the slide show, the tea ceremony. Then there was the time she grabbed his arm as the cage plunged down the mine shaft. Then the phone calls to the Vale when Ichiro was at work, the vast silence of the house save for the wind chimes.

She looked up at the sloping main road high above the reservoir and saw one of Ichiro's transporters, sleek in its blue-and-silver livery, catching the sun as it slid down from the hills towards the border with England. She could barely keep up with Ichiro's explanations of what was happening. She knew nothing could be done about his mother and her father, independently growing frail back home.

Every time Dr.Kagoshima came over, he reminded her with his hunched shoulders and his fine, thinning grey hair of the widow and widower, sitting silent in the groves of Wakamatsu. Shivering as the wind rattled down from the Heads of the Valleys, she wondered what Ichiro would think of her acting independently beyond the space he had created. What would anyone think, come to that ? On his first visit to the house, so long its heart-thumping excitement had been transferred to thoughts of the future, their future, Bill had warned of the perils of being a woman alone in a remote house, describing a Wales in which all slept with their doors bolted at night. She thought that her small size made him over-protective. They certainly made an odd-looking pair: he big and brawny yet considerate and gentle of voice; she for ever on tip-toe, as if peering over a ridge, the better to catch sight of some forbidden territory. Perhaps it was out of bounds because Ichiro had already identified places which would remind her of home, sites of gaping dereliction with kids mimicking aeroplanes in flight, just like the black, water-filled bumps of Nagasaki, where the aged saw their own ruination mirrored in the endless rubble.

She walked back to the car with her head bowed. Her tiny feet made scarcely a sound on the stones. Such lightness she felt now, as though she were disappearing into pure memory, out of the range of all that might do her harm. She and Bill had exchanged old photographs of themselves at one of the Home

Club's late sittings, while they waited for Ichiro to pick her up in his car, hers having broken down impressively. The Japanese wives had changed into Kimonos for the evening, and she recalled how the others had fluttered across the play area of the leisure centre, where the club's monthly hired room made perfect neutral ground among fellow learners. In one of the pictures, Bill was a lively nine year old, straining forwards as a snow-haired aunt held him in check for the photographer. Hers, too, were from an equally austere time. All was innocence then, in the days of struggle. As they shuffled the photos, passed them to each other and let them slip into a pile on the table between them, they took on the chaotic shape of destiny in the making. 'Little did they know,' she thought, 'little did they know.'

While waiting to pull out on to the main road, she thought she spotted one of the wives, there were just four of them in the district, driving in the opposite direction. Her heart quivered like a trapped bird. But it was too late to be worried about ostracism. In fact, she wished something like that would happen, some trickle of evidence to release the pressure of all her piled up guilt and frustration. She even cursed the old car as it laboured up the slope towards the Beacons, its low gears groaning. Ichiro's success had not made the other wives particularly friendly. As appendages of their go-getting husbands, they were saturated with the influence of ambition.

This was not the engagement with Western ways which she had yearned for as a girl; it was the old behaviour simply transferred to another place. In it she recognised the selfless but rough-shodden manner which, Bill said, had created so much ferment among the miners. He'd welcomed the arrival of Ichiro's factory but she knew when he had sighed so heavily at the museum's coalface, a huge black arrow-head caught pincer-like by crushing stone above and below, that reality was one thing but dignity quite another. Now that his workmates all wore blue overalls with their names on, it seemed easier to dispense with their services. She imagined someone ripping off the old tags and sewing on new ones.

At the Storey Arms, she parked in the lay-by opposite the hostel and read Bill's letter again. She ran her fingers over the clear, steady handwriting. He had addressed her as 'Dear Sachiko'. She remembered how someone had described Bill as a gentleman. What had this meant ? Discretion, good manners, consideration for the feelings of others ? All of these. In Nagasaki he would be considered a good match for someone like her. On the afternoon of his visit to the house, when Ichiro had phoned minutes earlier to say he had arrived safely in Doncaster for a meeting with Dr.Kagoshima, she almost crumbled under the weight of duplicity in a foreign land. Yet there was a peculiar thrill attached to its shared nature, as though it were a rite of passage to a higher plane of happiness. In Bill's embrace she might have been burying herself in the protective folds of the landscape he had commended to her with such pride of possession. She had lain on her bed in Nagasaki, reading of hills and vales and a people moved instinctively to song. 'Dear Sachiko,' Bill's letter said. 'We cannot go on. It's impossible. There's too much in the way.'

The long, worn path beckoned her to the summit. She closed her ears to the siren wind. How the other wives had giggled at the opera in Cardiff as Madame Butterfly tortured herself with ridiculous, old-fashioned feelings and Western music splashed everywhere like breakers from a strange sea. She balanced nervously at the edge of the escarpment and gazed into the void. Her arms shot out. In the gardens of Wakamatsu the trees shivered and a wheelchair turned sharply on a polished floor.